SCORCHED BY FATE

DRAKARN MATES
BOOK 3

KATE RUDOLPH

ONE
SELENE

Not all of the seven-foot-tall dragon men in Scalvaris were my type, especially not the one picking his nose with a wickedly sharp claw in the stall across the way.

The River Market stretched out ahead of me, loud and screaming with life—sometimes literally from the winged children running and flying wobbly around. Stalls packed with strange, deadly looking objects twisted along the stone paths, each one shouting for attention in ways that only reminded me how far from Earth we were.

Blades gleamed, crystals pulsed, and tangy-smelling smoke curled up from corners where food vendors flipped something that didn't look remotely edible. But this was life on Volcaryth—a mess of fire and survival. You didn't get to be picky.

I'd say we were the opposite of picky. Not a single one of us had *picked* this planet.

"Look at this!" Rachel Voss's voice cut through the noise. She stopped at a little stall draped in faded woven fabric, pointing at a series of pendants strung from a beam. "Am I wrong, or would this one match Kaiya's glasses *perfectly*?"

Kaiya frowned at the pendant and then at Rachel. "They're not a fashion statement. They're prescribed lenses."

Rachel laughed and rolled her eyes. She nudged me lightly with her elbow. "I don't remember anything in med school that prevented matching accessories."

Kaiya adjusted her thick glasses, clearly unimpressed. "What's the point? Now if you wanted to talk about the biodiversity of the materials and their potential similarities to—"

"Nope," Rachel interrupted before I could even open my mouth to weigh in. "There will be no science babble this early into the day. It's against the law."

"I must have missed that one," I said dryly. "And I think we've broken enough laws over the last three months." The dust was still settling from Orla and Rath's rather explosive mating and the sickening show they'd had to put on to prove themselves.

This earned the start of a grin from Rachel and an unimpressed sigh from Kaiya. I wasn't sure if I was proud or not for managing to keep the mood light. It wouldn't last long anyway. Not with Vega here.

She didn't have to say anything for me to know tension was brewing. With Vega, you could *feel* it first, like that second of silence after someone pulls a grenade pin. I clocked her pacing two stalls ahead of us, posture impossibly rigid. Still, I caught up to her. She'd made the effort to come out and be social.

"This is going to blow up in our faces," Vega muttered darkly. She wasn't looking at me as she spoke, but her voice had that razor-edge of judgment wrapped in thinly veiled exhaustion. "Those weird acolytes won't stop staring at us." She used her head to gesture further up the path to where three Drakarn in yellowish robes were not-so-subtly watching us shop.

Kaiya exchanged a glance with Rachel before pushing her glasses up her nose again. "They can watch us all they like. We're not doing anything wrong."

"Last I checked, we don't get to decide what's right or wrong," Vega said. She glanced warily at the yellow-robed acolytes. One of them—an older male with dark bronze scales—muttered something to his companion, and they both shifted, like they were debating whether to approach us. "They're not just watching. They're waiting."

Rachel scoffed. "Waiting for what?"

Vega scowled. "An excuse."

Rachel rolled her eyes and ignored her. "Say what you want," she said to Kaiya and me, her tone dipping into a teasing smirk, "but Drakarn biology does seem to kind of be working for some of us. Do you think their wingspan—"

"Seriously?" Vega hissed, spinning around to face Rachel like she'd just set fire to her common sense. "I'm over here worrying about execution orders, and you're busy ogling their damn wings?"

Unflustered, Rachel crossed her arms and tilted her head, smirking lazily. "I hear it's not just their wings."

"You're unbelievable," Vega grumbled, rubbing at her temple and clearly weighing whether or not she could strangle Rachel before any Drakarn noticed. If they would even care.

"Enough." This had to stop before they could land any more barbs. "We're not fighting in public." There were only ten humans in all of Scalvaris, on all of Volcaryth as far as we knew. We had to be a united front, or they'd tear us to shreds.

Rachel smirked again but didn't push it further.

Vega, on the other hand, scowled harder before turning and stomping out of the market, her steps brisk and just shy of furious.

Kaiya fell in step beside me as we continued deeper into the rows of alien wares. Her fingers twitched, as if itching to grab a sketchpad or start dissecting every new sight. "For the record," she said, her voice carefully neutral, "I'd still like to understand the biological implications."

I laughed under my breath. "I'm sure you can add it to your growing list of scientific obsessions."

Kaiya ducked her head, a hint of a blush creeping up her cheek. "I am a xenobiologist. I've spent my life studying alien life. This ... well, I never expected so much hands-on experience."

"Hands-on experience?" Rachel asked, a mischievous sparkle in her eye. "If you want hands-on with one of Scalvaris's finest, I'm sure I can arrange an introduction. I bet that guy over there has a tail for days. Very aerodynamic, I imagine."

"Why do I even try to have a serious conversation around any of you?" Kaiya muttered, her blush deepening as she adjusted her glasses for the third time. If she pressed them any harder against her nose, they'd probably fuse to her face.

I snorted, letting the banter run its course. Admittedly, it was nice to hear something other than discussions of survival plans and escape routes, even if the levity was probably doomed to be short-lived. Somewhere in the pit of my stomach, I could already feel the weight of Vega's earlier words.

She wasn't wrong. Execution orders or not, Scalvaris was a pressure cooker—and humans were just one more volatile ingredient thrown into the pot.

Before I could spiral too far, Rachel jerked her chin toward one of the stalls off to our left. "Check it out; that blade looks like some wizard shit."

The weapon on display was stunning. Long and curved ever-so-slightly, its edge gleamed with a sharpness that whispered deadly promises. Intricate heat crystals glowed along the hilt, the golden light flickering like trapped embers. The craftsmanship was undeniable.

It wasn't just a weapon; it was a masterpiece.

And it did look a little like something that could start shooting magic fireballs with the right words. But in my experience, aliens were real, magic? Not so much.

I stepped closer, letting my fingers hover just shy of the blade's surface. I wasn't stupid enough to touch it outright—some Drakarn got real tetchy about their goods being handled by strangers.

The vendor—an older Drakarn with scales the color of ash—leaned forward, his piercing orange gaze taking me in. "Admiring the fine work, human?" His voice rumbled low, carrying an edge of pride. Not threatening, which was refreshing for a change. Still, I straightened unconsciously, keeping my expression carefully neutral.

"It's ..." I faltered, searching for the right words. What could you even say about something this impressive? "It's beautiful. Did you ..."

The vendor's narrow pupils flicked from me to the weapon, a satisfied smile pulling at his lips. "It is the work of Vyne," he said, like that name alone should mean something to me. When I tilted my head, he chuckled. "One of our finest forge masters. His precision is unparalleled."

Vyne. I rolled the name around in my head, my brain immediately conjuring up the image of a certain Drakarn warrior I'd crossed paths with a few times—once in the healing caverns when I'd been learning from Mysha and again when he'd silently stepped in to help unload supplies without a word.

Dark green scales, broad shoulders, a face that could stop a woman in her tracks ... and hands as skilled as they were lethal.

Rachel's elbow nudged me lightly. "Oh no. I know that look."

I shot her a dry glance, shoving aside the very real mental image of Vyne, flickering forge light catching the sharp planes of his face. "I wasn't thinking about anything," I lied, struggling—and mostly failing—to sound convincing.

Rachel only smiled knowingly.

"Well, if you're interested," the vendor offered slyly, his scaled fingers drumming on the edge of his stall. "It's not often I have his blades to sell. He normally works on commission."

Words fizzled in my brain, refusing to form, which only fueled Rachel's growing amusement. She was going to hold this over my head for weeks.

Kaiya, probably sensing my rising discomfort, leaned forward to ask the vendor something about the heat crystals—her tone dripping with scientific curiosity. I was grateful for the diversion, but my mind had already run off on its own tangent, fixating on the absurdity of it all.

Strong hands. Precise craftsmanship. Quiet strength.

Damn it, Selene. Snap out of it.

If Vyne could pour that much focus and care into something like a blade, what else might he be capable of? What *would* it feel like to have those claws not carving metal but pressed gently to my skin, not as a weapon but—

Nope. Not going there.

I needed to get fucking laid. I'd joked about

having a Drakarn of my very own to Orla not long ago, but jokes were one thing. Inviting one of the dragon-men to my bed? I wasn't so sure.

I tore my gaze from the weapon and cleared my throat, forcing my attention back to my surroundings. The noise of the market seemed sharper now, every sound a little too loud as I tried to wrest control of my spiraling thoughts.

"It's getting late," I said briskly, cutting through Kaiya's excited chatter about living crystals. Rachel raised an eyebrow at me, clearly biting back another comment, but thankfully, she let it go.

The back of my neck itched like someone was watching me. I glanced backwards, looking for ... well, green scales if I was being honest. But if someone was watching me, they were doing it from the shadows.

Maybe this planet was getting to me after all.

TWO
VYNE

The market buzzed—too loud, too alive. I hovered at the edge of the chaos, half-draped in shadows. The crystals in the walls seemed to burn, casting fractured light over the crowd. It made their faces sharp, jagged, almost unreal.

Yet her face, among the other humans, stuck out like a spark waiting to catch.

A burst of laughter, human and soft, carried over rattling carts and shouted negotiations. The sound hit me like a blade, unfamiliar and fatally precise. My tongue ached, that strange sensitivity crawling up from the back of my throat and settling deep in my chest.

Selene.

For days ... longer than days if I was being honest, I'd been aware of her. Not actively—but in the way you notice the flare of forge-light in the dark, or the lingering echo of a hammer-strike after the sound fades. Today, she wasn't just another foreign presence in Scalvaris.

Today, something felt different.

I wouldn't be Rath, drawn in like a moth to fire despite knowing how it would scorch. I was sharper than that. My sense of self-preservation still had teeth.

But when she laughed again, my body betrayed me, dragging my gaze toward their group. Four of them together, a tight-knit cluster navigating the crowd with cautious joy. They moved like a flock of sunglow finches, all darting movements and quiet giggles bound by instinctive camaraderie. They were softer than anything else in the market. Their fragility was jarring, delicate within the sharp angles of Scalvaris.

Delicate, but not weak.

Her hair caught my attention first. Light caught the strands as she tilted her head toward another of the women, listening intently to their conversation. A smirk tugged at the corner of her lips. A quiet predator, watching and observing before striking with some dry quip, I wagered.

It wasn't her beauty, though she had enough of it to snap a weaker male's resolve. It wasn't the way she tucked her hands close to her chest when a small Drakarn child ran past her clutching sticky scales of stolen candy. And it damn well wasn't the slight upward curve of her jawline showing off the tension in her neck as her smirk relaxed back into something unreadable.

It was her scent—a phantom warmth that lingered on the smoke-filled air. Something sweet, slightly sharp underneath, like phoenix fruit steeped in herb oil. The scent tightened every nerve in my body, wild yanking at my restraint.

My tongue tingled again, sharper this time, as if some unseen force had lashed it. It made me want to step forward, part the crowd surrounding them, and inhale until my chest finally stopped burning.

I retreated deeper into the shadows, claws twitching uselessly at my sides. What was this, exactly? Was it the same tethering madness that had dragged Rath through the hells for his human? That had made Darrokar act like a fool?

I clenched my jaw, the barbell in my tongue clicking against my teeth. Whatever it was, it needed to stop.

Rath had barely survived the upheaval caused by his bond. He'd fought tooth and claw against Karyseth and the vultures circling Scalvaris's politics.

I didn't have his patience or his recklessness. I'd

spent most of my life artfully dancing just under the council's scrutiny, dodging unnecessary risks and skulking out of the spotlight.

Her laughter cut through me again, raw as an open wound. It scraped away the pretense I clung to, the false calm I'd worn like armor for so long.

I was supposed to be good at ignoring stupid ideas. At looking through the fire and thinking about my next move. But suddenly, I was back at the edge of the market without realizing my feet had moved. The women were still there, farther ahead now, lingering near a vendor draped with polished obsidian necklaces. She stood apart from her companions, fingers pressed to a lichen-brushed gemstone, her expression thoughtful.

The ache twisted tighter. My tail jerked in protest, smacking a low crate behind me with a crack, forcing me to snap it controlled again.

"Fucking idiot," I hissed under my breath.

To her, from a distance, I probably looked no better than some skulking stalker with half a brain.

But she didn't notice me. No one did—not even the vendor, who was preoccupied arguing with another Drakarn over the price of lava-lizard talons decorated in intricate painted patterns. It was easy to slip closer. Close enough to see the drag marks in the dust where her boots had scuffed the ground. Close enough to think about reaching out ... for what, I didn't even know.

The scent hit me harder then. Impossible not to notice when it wrapped around me like a second skin, pulling me in like the currents of an underground river. My tongue burned red hot, every sensitive tastebud lighting up with phantom flavor.

It would be so easy to close the distance. To press clawed fingers lightly to her shoulder so she'd turn. To watch as her wide, unfamiliar human eyes took me in. To speak—just one word, a name, her name. Or to say nothing at all and just let the silence stretch between us, burning this unnatural pull into the fabric of what could become ...

Would become nothing.

I dragged the thought back, sharp as my blades. Nothing. No "could," no "would."

A mate—a *human*—wasn't something I could claim. Not now, not ever. Karyseth's schemes against Rath and Orla proved that truth well enough.

Why would I want to give her another opening? Rath and Orla had already survived enough. I wasn't about to play with lava after their fragile truce.

Something in me hardened as I stepped away again, the ache in my chest twisting into something closer to a wound.

Self-inflicted. Necessary.

I turned, setting my path deliberately away from the market's packed heart. "Be smarter than him, you idiot," I muttered to the emptiness ahead. I repeated it like a mantra, the words as bitter as sand trapped under my tongue.

Be smarter than Rath. Be smarter.

But even as I turned my back on her, I swore I could still taste the way her scent lingered on the grit-flavored air.

And the burn wouldn't subside.

THREE
SELENE

The forge was a beast.

Heat slammed into me the second I stepped inside, thick and heavy enough to drown in. It burrowed under my skin, snagged in my lungs, a dare to even try and breathe. The noise was a physical assault—hammer on metal, the shriek of steam.

Mercy for sensitive ears or headaches? Forget about it.

Definitely not my happy place.

Sweat already slicked the back of my neck as I crossed the threshold. Mysha's list was crumpled tight in my hand, a knot of worry cinching tight in my chest. The elder healer's fainting spell from earlier wouldn't leave me alone, even if she'd snapped at me and waved me off like it was normal. I wasn't buying it. Not after that glimpse of her hands —bruises under the scales, faint and mottled.

Something was wrong, and it wasn't just her temper.

The noise clanged louder, deeper, as I moved farther into the cavern. Tables overflowed with tools, metal scraps, and surprisingly delicate sketches of blades pinned to the rough rock walls. Chaos, but organized chaos. Everything had its place, even if it looked like a disaster to anyone else. I got the symmetry of it, even as I edged around things that looked sharp enough to slice me open by accident.

Then I saw him.

Dead center in the forge's heart. Heat and fire-light framed him like he'd clawed his way out of the flames themselves. Broad shoulders, green scales catching shadows of black, wings folded back but still massive. He moved like he was born to this, hammer rising and falling on a glowing blade, muscles flexing under his scales with each strike. His focus was a laser, locked on the metal as if daring it to disobey.

I stopped at the edge of his space, shifting my weight. Underneath the worry for Mysha, I was suddenly too aware of being an outsider. Even more than usual. The forge was *his* territory. I was just ...

human and wrapped up in human problems he probably couldn't care less about.

I cleared my throat, voice quiet against the forge's roar. "Vyne."

He didn't falter, hammer still in its rhythm, but his eyes flicked up. Sharp, slit pupils narrowed as they found me. His chest rose in a controlled breath, a flicker of irritation crossing his face before it smoothed out. Neutral. Not friendly, not warm. Just ... less annoyed.

"You're early," he said, voice rough as rocks grinding together. The hammer came down one last time, then he plunged the blade into a shallow pool of liquid. Steam hissed up, like an angry spirit escaping.

I arched a brow, holding up Mysha's wrinkled list. "I didn't realize there was a schedule."

A ghost of a smirk touched the corner of his mouth. It didn't quite make it all the way. He tossed the hammer onto the workbench, the clang echoing and making me wince.

"Let me see it." Hand out, palm up, claws twitching. I hesitated for a beat. But he didn't owe me a kind tone. I stepped closer and held out the crumpled list.

His fingers brushed mine as he took it, and one word slammed into my brain before I could block it—

warm. Too warm. Hot actually. Like fire licking skin, but without the burn, just that unsettling, sharp pleasure that faded too fast. Vyne's touch was … something else.

Something dangerous.

I snatched my hand back, tucked it behind me like it had suddenly betrayed me. He didn't seem to notice. Or care. His attention was glued to the list, eyes narrowed at the scribbled handwriting.

"Is Mysha trying to kill me with this?" he muttered after a second, tilting the paper like that would magically decode it.

I bit back a laugh. "I'm pretty sure her penmanship is worse than her bedside manner." I was still struggling to learn to read the Drakarn language. My translator made speaking easy. Reading Mysha's handwriting was like trying to decipher hieroglyphics.

That got a low huff of amusement.

"Half of this is gibberish," he grumbled, squinting harder at the messy script. "You sure she didn't spatter ink on the paper and call it good?"

"I wouldn't rule it out." I folded my arms, shifted my weight. The forge was roasting, but the back-and-forth made it almost pleasant. "But she wouldn't ask for anything we didn't need."

"Since when is it a we?"

I bristled. "I've been training with Mysha since we got here." No need to specify when. To say that me and my fellow humans had made a splash in Scalvaris was an understatement.

Vyne's head tilted, and I caught a flicker of something almost ... soft ... in his expression. Wry. Maybe even amused. Then it was gone, locked back behind the hard lines of his face.

"It'll take time," he finally said, rolling the list into a loose tube and setting it on his bench. "Some of this is ... finicky. The apprentices can handle most of it, but I'll have to tackle this," he pointed to one indecipherable line, "myself."

"And here I was, thinking you'd have it all ready by yesterday," I deadpanned, arching a brow.

That ghost-smirk again. Not quite softening, but there. "I'll have an apprentice get started on what's available. The rest might take a few days."

His gaze flicked to me again, sharp and assessing, and heat crept up my neck. Maybe it was just the forge finally getting to me. Yeah, probably that.

"Thank you," I said, ignoring the tightness in my throat. "Mysha's not exactly patient. But I'll pass it on. If she's not happy, she can fly down here and complain herself."

That earned a snort—a real one this time. His wings shifted, rustling in the heated air. "I'd like to see her try," he muttered, then inclined his head toward the doorway. "You should get moving before the heat does more than just flush you pink."

I jolted and damn it if my cheeks didn't get even pinker.

When I looked up, there was something in his gaze—not exactly indecent, but *knowing*. Too knowing. Like he'd noticed more than just the heat getting to me. My flushed skin, the way I couldn't seem to stop glancing at his hands.

Damn those hands.

The last thing I needed was to start imagining what they might feel like against my skin. And the rest of him?

Damn it again.

I cleared my throat, nodded, and turned, getting out of there before I could embarrass myself further. But even walking away, I could feel his stare. His eyes tracked me across the forge, a pressure on my back I didn't want to think too hard about. I bit the inside of my cheek, focusing on putting one foot in front of the other until I was past the threshold, back in the blessedly cooler tunnels.

I blew out a breath, dragging a hand over my damp forehead. My heart was still hammering, too fast, like I'd just escaped a fight. Except it wasn't fear driving my pulse. It was something sharper. I didn't want to name it, but I wasn't stupid.

A male like Vyne, he pulled you in, even if you fought to stay *out*.

I didn't need this. Not now.

I forced my thoughts back on track. Mysha. The list. The illness that had her leaning against the wall earlier like standing upright was too much effort.

By the time I reached the healing caverns, the tension in my chest had eased a little. Whatever had been fighting for my attention in the forge had no place here.

Something had been wrong for days. A tension in the air, a sluggishness in the way some of the healers moved. Mysha had been snapping at apprentices more than usual, rubbing her temples like even the dim cavern light was too much.

The orderly calm I associated with the Drakarn healers, their smooth efficiency, their collected focus, was fractured. Whispers, low and urgent, volleyed over prone bodies. Fabric rustled; muffled gasps and groans filled the air.

I froze just inside the entrance as the picture snapped into focus, sharp and ugly.

Mysha wasn't the only one sick.

Two other healers lay nearby, sprawled like they'd collapsed mid-step. The strange bruises weren't faint marks now—they spread dark and web-like across their calves and arms. A few other Drakarn moved through the room, jerky and clumsy, eyes glazed, clawed hands fumbling with supplies they couldn't seem to manage.

Rachel was crouched over one of the healers, brow furrowed in concentration. Kaiya moved between makeshift tables with frantic energy, her tension leaking out in sharp, tight movements.

"Selene!" Rachel's head snapped up as soon as I moved farther inside. Her voice was loud, sharp, but controlled enough to cut through the chaos. "Get over here. The shit hit the fan."

"What the hell happened?" I asked, crouching next to the closest Drakarn, not touching yet, just observing. Their chest barely lifted, shallow breaths that didn't seem to suck in enough air. The bruising was darker, spreading out from their torso. Veins under the scales were raised and angry. Beside them, bandages soaked in a green residue lay useless in a bowl of water that had somehow turned murky.

Rachel shook her head, standing, wiping her hands on her pants as she came closer. "Mysha collapsed just after you left. Then Sharyth and Nyzarin. It's spreading too fast to track. Symptoms are all over the place—muscle spasms in one, vascular issues in another. And I have no idea what's causing it. Kaiya's been consulting her notes, but we don't know *anything*."

"So the universe is being a bastard again." It came out harsher than I meant, but I wasn't there for soft words and handholding.

Kaiya spoke before Rachel could, appearing at my side, strung tight with tension. "We need samples. Data, patient histories," she said, voice clipped but precise. "Maybe they were exposed to something ... specific. Or maybe this is a known disease. I was trying to compare what I know about—"

"Kaiya," I interrupted, fixing her with my no-nonsense look, the one for when things were going sideways and we were out of time for theories. "Focus. What's workable now?"

To her credit, she didn't flinch, though her fingers twitched, betraying the battle to hold back the flood of ideas in her head. "Rachel's doing triage, trying to stabilize vitals. I tried a microdose of Earth antibiotics, just to rule out—"

"Good," I cut her off again, not unkindly. Focus was Kaiya's lifeline and reeling her back when she got lost in her own thoughts was part of the deal. "Stick to what's working. Rachel—"

I turned to her as she packed another vial into her med kit, sharp eyes already scanning the room like she could fix it with sheer will. "Did Mysha give us any hints?"

Rachel's lips tightened. "No. She's unconscious now, same as the others. Her symptoms are getting worse." Her gaze flicked to the makeshift triage area, the cot where Mysha lay still, face pinched even in sleep.

It took effort to keep panic out of my voice. "Do we need contamination protocols? Any signs it's jumping species?"

Rachel paused, weighing her answer. "Nothing yet. We're exposed, obviously, but we seem ... unaffected. So far."

"Not exactly comforting," I muttered, already pulling gloves from the kit and snapping them on. My hands moved on autopilot, finding the pulse at the neck of the nearest healer.

Weak, thready. Fuck.

I glanced around again, the harsh light bouncing off hollow cheeks and ragged breaths. The air felt thicker, pressing on my lungs like the forge, but this was worse. The forge was simple heat. This was ... hell.

"Alright," I barked, pulling my voice sharp, the tone they responded to because it sounded like I had a plan. I didn't. Not yet. But I'd fake it until I did.

"Rachel, keep triage going. Airway stabilization first, and—"

"God damn it." Rachel's voice was dry, almost flat. I followed her gaze across the room to a younger healer clawing at the wall, movements twitchy and frantic, like he was trying to rip something invisible out of his own body. Then, like his strings were cut, he crumpled, face-first on the floor.

"Shit," I hissed, already moving, but Rachel's hand shot out, hard on my shoulder. "Bad idea," she said, firm.

"No choice," I snapped. "We have to contain this."

"You touch him, we risk exposure."

That stopped me. For about a second.

"We're already fucking exposed," I said, fierce, crossing my arms despite the growing weight in my chest. "Not touching him doesn't magically make us safe, Rachel," I continued, voice dropping harder, colder than I usually let it get. "We control what we can, or we watch everyone in this room die."

FOUR
SELENE

One Week Later

It smelled like sickness. Like death.

My boots scuffed against the stone floor as I darted from one makeshift quarantine area to the next, eyes scanning for any signs of change in the afflicted healers.

Drakarn who had once stood tall and composed now sagged against stone benches, their scaled bodies limp and marked with angry, festering sores. Most barely moved. Some didn't move at all. The only sound they made was a wheeze, too weak to cough or cry out.

A creeping ache settled low in my gut at the sight, but I pushed it down. I'd been learning Drakarn healing ways for weeks, and now ...

Focus.

The murmurs and steady rhythm of the healing caverns were gone. Instead, rushed footsteps, clipped voices, and the scraping of trays across stone replaced normalcy. My throat tightened from the acrid sting in the air, something chemical and *wrong* that we couldn't identify. The healers were dropping like stones, and nothing seemed to be stopping it.

"Kaiya, double-check the gear for all the humans. Vega, I need this entire section cordoned off—no one without protection gets near it. Rachel, go through the patient notes again. We must've missed something."

I wasn't a doctor, and I'd never felt it more than now. But as a combat medic, I understood triage.

And some of the Drakarn definitely wouldn't make it.

Kaiya's anxious nod and Vega's sharp grunt of acknowledgment were quick—exactly what I needed. They moved, figures cutting through the flickering light of the caverns. Rachel hunched over Mysha, her hand hovering over the elder's still form before quickly moving to assess her vitals.

The head healer hadn't stirred in hours.

I crouched beside a young Drakarn who had collapsed earlier, inspecting the inflamed sores spreading along his throat. My gloved fingers pressed near the edge of one on his neck. The swollen lump gave slightly beneath the pressure, and a thin trail of yellowish fluid leaked out. It was wrong.

It didn't behave like anything I'd seen before, but it also reminded me of far too many things. This was an alien disease on an alien planet. I wished for a computer, a research book, *anything* that might give me a clue to what we were dealing with.

"We need to keep them hydrated," I said quietly, the words more for myself than anyone else. I turned to Rachel. "This isn't just lethargy. None of them have shown a real thirst response, even now."

"We're handling fluids," Rachel replied steadily, but the tightness around her mouth betrayed her apprehension.

In another area of the hall, Orla was trying to rig brighter lighting using salvaged human tech. Her muttered curses reached me even from here. Every single human on Scalvaris, all ten of us, as if that was anything, was involved in trying to keep the healers alive. I didn't want this disease spreading to the Drakarn in the city. So far, us humans seemed immune.

Movement from the perimeter caught my attention. Vega pushed back a Drakarn warrior who had ventured too close, her hand planted firmly against his chest. I stood just as her voice rose, clear and firm.

"Stay back," she snapped, her posture rigid. "We

don't know what's causing this yet or how it spreads. Do you want to risk carrying it through the city?"

The warrior growled something low, his tail flicking in agitation, but he didn't argue when Vega jabbed a gloved finger toward a nearby guard post. He backed away with a sharp lash of annoyance.

"Good," I called out tersely. "Keep it that way."

Vega glanced at me over her shoulder, and I could see the tension in her. She trusted exactly no one right now, and I couldn't say I blamed her. But aggression wouldn't help, either. I walked toward her as I pulled off my gloves to swap them for a fresh pair from the kit at my belt.

"Don't be too hard on them," I muttered as I passed her. "We'll get better cooperation if you're not threatening to shank anyone who breathes near us."

She crossed her arms. "Cooperation isn't going to help if this spreads."

I paused but only for a moment. "Noted."

Kaiya was carrying a tray of cleaned medical tools repurposed from both Drakarn and human supplies. The hybrid assortment made my stomach twist. Most of these were improvised; none of them were right for what we needed there. I examined the tray, my movements brisk, but the frustration gnawed at me.

Too clunky. Too wide. Scalpel edges dulled.

Forceps too large for precise work. The designs of their tools weren't suited for the nuanced procedures we needed to treat a condition like this. They were weapons repurposed for healing, without the finesse required for something this delicate. My hands hovered over the instruments, imagining the strain of trying to use these on something like infected glands or necrotic tissue. I forced down a sharp exhale.

What we had wasn't enough, and what we needed ... Damn it.

"I'll be back," I told Kaiya before stalking towards the decontamination station and out of the caverns.

The forge wasn't far. Its heat seeped into the tunnels leading there, wrapping around me with the oppressive weight of the magma that flowed through the heart of Volcaryth. I was practically running, Drakarn dodging out of my way as I took corners too fast and nearly flung myself into a wall in my haste.

We needed better tools to stand a chance against whatever this thing was.

A disease? Poison? Parasite?

When I stepped into the forge's main chamber, the world tilted. The air was thicker there, throbbing with the energy of molten metal and the clanging of hammer on steel. Forge masters worked in silence, their movements fluid. But it wasn't them that drew my focus.

It was him.

Vyne stood at the far end of the forge, his back to me. Broad shoulders framed by wings flexed as he adjusted the angle of his anvil.

He worked with a focused intensity, his clawed hands guiding a thin blade under the precise heat of a Drakarn forge light. Shadows flickered across the lines of his emerald scales, giving them a deeper shine that caught coppery hues buried beneath the green. I didn't have time to notice, but my body didn't care what my brain was trying to do.

His scent hit me like a caress—subtle, warm, and irritatingly familiar even though we barely knew each other. But now, in the thick heat of the forge, it surrounded him like a second skin.

My tongue tingled, and I swallowed hard, pushing the feeling away, even as my body burned from more than the heat of the forge. My fingers ached to reach out for him. Clearly, exhaustion and stress were getting to me.

This wasn't the time or place.

"Vyne," I called out, keeping my voice steady as I stepped into the sweltering forge chamber.

His back was to me, broad and unyielding, but his movements faltered for the briefest moment. The metallic ring of his hammer paused mid-strike before

picking up again, slower this time, as if he were delib-
erating something. He didn't turn.

"What are you doing here, human?" he said, his
voice gruff, like gravel scraping against steel. "I had
an apprentice deliver everything you asked for."

I crossed the stone floor, ignoring the heat
clawing at my skin and the prickle of awareness
under it. The Drakarn had a way of making you feel
like you didn't belong, but I wasn't about to let him
push me out. Not when lives were at stake.

"The healers are collapsing," I said bluntly,
cutting past any pleasantries. "Mysha's sick. Whatever's hitting them is spreading fast, and we have
nothing precise enough to work with. I need tools
that aren't clumsy, that fit human hands. I need you."

His hammer froze mid-strike, the unfinished
blade glowing beneath his claws.

Slowly, he turned, towering over me even across
the modest distance between us. The flickering glow
of molten fires caught the ridges of his scaled face,
sharpening every detail—the scar cutting through his
left brow, the flick of his tail that betrayed his
thoughts more than his stoic expression did.

His yellow eyes locked onto mine, and it felt like
the air in the forge shifted. Heavy. Different.

"You need *me*?" he repeated slowly, with just
enough skepticism to make me grit my teeth.

"I need your tools," I corrected, stressing the word. This wasn't time for games. "You're the best forge master in the city, aren't you? I've seen your work. You're ... precise. Fast. And that's what I need right now."

If my words flattered him, his face didn't show it. That cold, assessing gaze stayed fixed on me, searching, like he was looking for the real reason I had walked into *his* forge and demanded his skills. The silence stretched a little too long, the heat of the room pressing down on me harder by the second.

"I don't know what's causing it," I continued, softening slightly, "but I know we can't treat it with what we have. I need finer instruments."

His jaw tightened, and for a second, I thought he'd sneer and shrug me off. But then his gaze shifted, lingering on me just a beat too long before he finally exhaled through his nose.

"What exactly do you need?" he asked curtly, moving toward a nearby workbench without waiting for me to answer.

The tension in my chest loosened, and I stepped closer, the air between us feeling too charged and strangely fragile.

"Fine-tipped forceps, micro-serrated scalpels, tools precise enough to work between scale and muscle without damage," I said quickly, listing off items as I pictured the mess in the healing halls. "Retractors shaped for Drakarn anatomy, articulated probes—"

The faintest quirk of his brow stopped me mid-word. His eyes glinted with something unreadable—sharp, calculating, and maybe a little irritated.

"You speak like someone who's spent too much time thinking about my blades," he muttered, grabbing a chunk of heat-resistant alloy and turning it over in his hand.

For a moment, my tongue tied. The way he said it, quiet and under his breath, made something in my stomach twist.

"I've spent a lot of time thinking about saving lives," I corrected, shaking off whatever weird feeling tried to crawl up my spine. I clenched my hands into fists at my sides. "You can forge these, can't you?"

He snorted, almost amused, as he dropped the alloy onto the workbench and reached for another. "I can forge anything. Question is whether your humans know how to use what I make ... or if you're just wasting my time."

I bristled, taking another step forward. "It's wasting time to talk like this when people are dying. You want to sit here and mock humans while the sickness spreads through *your* kind?"

The flare of defiance in my own voice caught me off guard, but I didn't step back.

Finally, Vyne's gaze softened—barely. Just enough for his brow to furrow instead of sneer as his claws dragged across the table's surface with a sharp rasp.

"You'll have them by dawn," he said, finally. Then he turned back to the forge, dismissing me entirely.

Even as relief coursed through me, I didn't move right away. I couldn't, not with the crackling heat of the room lingering in my lungs and his scent digging into senses I didn't know could react so strongly.

I exhaled sharply, ripping my attention back to the reason I'd come here in the first place.

The healers. Focus on the healers.

"Good," I said stiffly, already angling back toward the exit. "Don't make me chase you down for them."

FIVE
VYNE

Hammer struck metal. The sound echoed all around the forge, ringing in my ears. I forced rhythm into the chaos, controlling each movement. The forge's heat clawed at my scales—hot even for a Drakarn—but I didn't let myself pause. Each strike burned more energy into the tools taking shape beneath my claws.

Forceps. Scalpel. Something articulated, precise.

These weren't weapons. But the urgency was the same.

Sweat gathered along the edges of my scales as the tools inched closer to completion. The alloy's glow dimmed under the shaping, its heat yielding to my control, but not without resistance. Each adjustment demanded focus, every shift a test of my patience. My claws twitched against the metal.

The ache of tension rippled through my chest again, sharp as the scent that had refused to leave my senses since she was there. It lingered in my head, maddening and intrusive. I clenched my jaw hard enough to make the barbell in my tongue press into the roof of my mouth.

My hammer didn't slow. Letting it stop would mean letting those thoughts in.

Her voice had settled into the forge, too. Not its tone—no, that was already fading from memory. What clung to me was its edge. A command without invitation. A sharpness that didn't back down, born of necessity, not arrogance.

I growled low, pressing the blade of my hammer against the edge of the forming scalpel to narrow its contour. Self-preservation urged me to scrub every trace of her from my mind. But self-preservation was never good at winning when instinct screamed its demands. Not with her scent still burning through the air.

This was ridiculous.

The forge cracked around me, molten currents bubbling beneath reinforced grates. Time blurred as I moved from one tool to the next. The hiss of metal bending was the only sound louder than my rhythm. The edges of tools sharpened, taking clearer shapes like whispers pulled into focus.

I thought of her hands as I crafted. Smaller than a Drakarn's; the adjustments for human size needed precision finer than I liked. It had been hard enough to balance efficiency with my usual sense of perfection. Now it was harder with her face flashing through my memory in brief, cutting fractures.

Focused. Strong.

Her face wasn't supposed to linger. But it did.

Selene.

The tips of my claws scratched against cooled metal as I set the last tool down on my anvil. My breathing steadied slowly, and I stood there a moment longer than I needed to.

The ache took root again, curling beneath my ribs like it had always been there, and I fought the urge to smash the nearest unfinished blade to pieces just for the brief release it might bring.

It had been this way for weeks now. Ever since Rath's situation had nearly killed him and his mate, I'd kept my distance. Seeing how it had nearly drowned him—and brought chaos to all of Scalvaris besides—should've quenched any flame before it started.

But no matter how many walls I built in my mind, Selene's scent hit them like a battering ram.

I looked at the finished tools on the anvil. The

glow of their tempered steel mirrored the heat crawling through my chest. This wasn't about her.

This was about the work.

About the healers, and whatever sickness clawed them down like prey picked apart by stealthy predators.

I gathered the tools into a sturdy leather wrap, folding it with care. My movements were efficient, detached. Anything to keep my thoughts chained to the task, not to *her*. The ache still gnawed in my chest.

The path to the healing caverns was quiet. News of the sickness was spreading, and healthy Drakarn were keeping their distance. Only the occasional flicker of heat crystals lit my path, their light fractured and uneven. My grip tightened on the bundle of tools.

When I entered the cavern, the stench of sickness assaulted my senses, burning against the cool edge of healing salves and sterilized metal. The space buzzed with tension, low murmurs from humans and the occasional rasp of a dying breath filtering through the stillness.

Selene was at the center of it all, moving with quick precision. Her black hair was tied back, stray strands sticking to her damp skin as she worked. She was bent over a table, inspecting a makeshift chart pinned to the surface, her hand stilling against the edge of it as she processed something. Her expression was stone—you'd think she wasn't panicking. But her hand tensed, small but unmistakable, and I saw the edge of fatigue carving its place into her jawline.

She needed to rest. I wanted to rush in and demand she return to her chambers, or, better yet, mine, and sleep until the darkness faded from under her eyes.

I had no right.

A Drakarn guard jostled past me, his tail narrowly avoiding my own. I didn't move.

She hadn't noticed me yet.

Part of me wanted to leave. To set the tools down and vanish before she turned, before her eyes met mine and triggered that ache that refused to burn out. But my feet ignored me, carrying me farther into the cavern until my shadow stretched across her table.

Her head snapped up at the movement, dark eyes flicking toward me. For a second, relief flickered across her face, subdued but unmistakable. "That was fast."

"Done ahead of schedule." The words came out

sharper than I meant, their edge sinking into the air between us. My claws flexed against the tool wrap. "Are the healers still alive?"

She gave me that tight, no-nonsense look, the one that made it annoyingly difficult to shake her off. "Barely," she said, her tone clipped but calm. Her hands reached out as I lowered the bundle onto the table.

She unwrapped the tools with care, fingers running over each one like she was memorizing their shapes. The forceps, the scalpel, the retractors. Her focus stayed on the metal, her lips pressed into a line of concentration.

"These are ..." Her voice trailed off before she glanced up at me again. "This is ... good."

I didn't reply. The gratitude in her tone should've been satisfying. It wasn't.

I wanted more.

Her fingers lingered over the scalpel, testing its balance, its weight. She set it down carefully, her eyes finally lifting to mine.

"You didn't have to deliver these yourself," she said, and there was no accusation in her voice. Only curiosity.

"I needed to stretch my legs," I muttered, crossing my arms. My own excuse felt weak, even to my ears.

Her gaze narrowed, assessing me in a way that turned the air between us heavier than the forge's heat. She nodded, an arch of her brow betraying amusement. "Thank you, really. But you need to leave now."

I snorted. "So soon?"

Her expression was grave. "Whatever this is, it spreads fast."

That brief flicker of relief was gone. Now it was all focus again, all energy coiled into tension she wouldn't let herself release. Watching her was like watching an arrow pulled back too tightly against its bowstring.

I should've turned and left. I didn't.

Instead, I stepped closer, forcing her to look up again. My claws tapped once—twice—on the edge of the table. "If you're short on hands, I'll help."

Her eyes widened, only for a moment before she tilted her head back to that same assessing stare. "We have this under control for now."

I was close enough now to pick out the scent clinging to her again. Krysfruit soap. Smoke laced within it. Something sharper, too, adrenaline-laced, lingering just above her skin. The ache I'd melted into the tools roared back, uncontained.

I wanted to argue. I had no business here, nothing but rudimentary knowledge of how to treat wounds in the field. But I spotted at least half of the humans in Scalvaris tending to Drakarn, and exhaustion was dragging at each and every one of them.

If they didn't find a way to treat this illness soon, they'd be the ones in need of help.

"Let me know if you need more tools," I said. As if that was sufficient.

Selene nodded, and I was dismissed.

When I stepped back into the tunnels, the air shifted again. Colder. Stale. Yet I still swore I could taste her on every inhale, as if leaving the caverns hadn't been enough to escape the burn.

THE COUNCIL WAS RESTLESS. And scared.

Never a good combination.

Mektar stood near the central table, wings tucked tight against his back, his shadow sharp. Zarvash lingered at the far end, hunched over one of his maps as always, his claws tapping idly against the surface. Khorlar's broad frame towered over the others, his stone-gray scales making him an even grimmer fixture against the firelit backdrop. Darrokar and Rath spoke to one another in hushed tones.

I didn't like the stiffness in the room. It promised nothing good.

Mektar didn't waste time.

"The humans," he snarled, voice low and biting. His midnight-blue scales caught silver streaks from the heat crystals as his tail jerked behind him, one curved claw tapping in measured strokes against the stone. "Their presence. Their interference. And now, their poison."

I stiffened. My claws curled at my sides, but I forced restraint into my voice. "Poison?"

Mektar's expression darkened further. He turned slightly, angling his body toward the central table as if expecting allies to rise from the shadows of the chamber. "Do you think it's coincidence this sickness began now? That Mysha herself—an elder—has fallen? We are not blind, Vyne. The Forge Temple—"

Rath groaned. "The Forge Temple sees enemies in every shadow."

My jaw twitched. Mektar's voice grated on every nerve I had grown tired of sanding down. "The humans have no more idea what caused this than we do," I said, my tone flat and edged in mirthless humor. "But yes, brilliant theory. Let's assume they crashed landed on our planet, waited several months, attempted to integrate into our society, and then whipped up an illness targeting our people, all while volunteering themselves to die along the way. Master strategists, clearly."

Sarcasm coated the words like molten slag, and I didn't bother softening it. Mektar shot me a glare. His claws scraped louder against the table as his tail flicked erratically. "Their weakness invites sickness! Their blood carries it! They are frail creatures, and whatever infects them spreads faster than wildfire. Shall we wait until it has taken root in each of us before acting?"

"Is that an actual question?" I asked lightly, leaning back on one foot. "Because while we're slinging paranoid accusations, perhaps you should consider someone more credible. Anyone from the Temple make an unannounced visit lately? Say, to the healing caverns? To stir things up a bit, as they tend to enjoy doing?"

Zarvash's brow quirked at that—subtle, but there —and Mektar's expression darkened. For all his bristling and righteous indignation, the accusation landed just close enough to the truth to irritate him. His wings flared before snapping back against his spine.

"You think the Forge Temple would harm our healers?" Mektar sneered, brushing the words aside like ashes in the wind. He was trying too hard. "The Forge Temple stands to protect our people's traditions, not poison them."

"Of course," I said dryly, crossing my arms. "I'm

sure that's precisely what they're thinking when half their low-ranked acolytes hound Rath, screaming about divine judgment because he claimed a mate. Very hospitable. Truly guardians of reason and decency."

Rath let out a short bark of laughter from the other end of the room, and even Zarvash couldn't stop the twitch of his lips that threatened to resemble approval. Mektar's irritation boiled over, his claws leaving visible divots in the table now.

"Enough foolishness!" Mektar growled, glaring across the room like he was daring anyone to challenge him outright. "The Blade Council should stand united in protecting Scalvaris—not indulging in childish deflections. The Forge Temple—whether you agree with their methods or not—speaks to the heart of this matter. We should listen."

Rath rolled his eyes so hard I thought his head might snap backward. "Oh, absolutely. We should let the priests guide our survival. Maybe throw a few humans into the lava while we're at it, just to cleanse their 'weak blood.' Who shall we start with? Darrokar's mate? Mine?"

Darrokar growled.

Mektar snarled in response, but before he could launch into whatever drivel passed for a counterargument, Zarvash clapped his hands once, the sound sharp even in the fire-lit chamber.

"Enough," Zarvash said coolly, his tone slicing through the tension with a dangerous calm that carried no room for argument. He tilted his head, keen gaze sweeping across Mektar before settling briefly on me. "Mektar, do not be foolish. The humans did not spread this disease. And you, Vyne, know the Temple would do no such thing. We've wasted enough time chasing our tails. Here is what we know: The humans' quarantine methods are working—for now. Their intervention has stopped any spread into the city. The humans seem to be immune to whatever is causing this."

His words had just enough venom to make Mektar twitch again, but Zarvash didn't stop. "If we exile the humans now, what exactly do we gain? Crippling fear? Spreading this sickness? I don't want them here any more than you do, but it would be foolish to punish them now for helping."

Zarvash, the voice of reason. Since when?

From this angle, I could see Mektar's claws tap against the stone, too forceful to be casual. "Maybe we should form a committee," I offered, my voice perfectly bland. "One to vote on who gets to deal with the crisis first: the humans with brains and solutions, or the Temple with prayers and sacrifice. I'd love to see how those results come back."

Mektar hissed under his breath, his glare cutting toward me more murderous than it had been all night. "You tread too close to heresy, Vyne."

I exhaled through my nose, unbothered. "If heresy means valuing practicality over fanaticism, allow me to fetch the shackles myself."

Zarvash made a sound halfway between a sigh and a laugh, low and exasperated but not without amused acknowledgment. He straightened, fixing his gaze once more on the room's larger audience, deliberately dragging the focus away from me and Mektar before the latter self-combusted.

"If we intend to approach this situation *logically*," Zarvash said once more, with renewed emphasis, "then I suggest no more delays. Order additional supplies drawn from the lower stores. Work with the humans—not against them—to analyze the sickness's source and treatment. Above all, ensure cooperation, or risk this disease spreading throughout the city."

The silence that followed wasn't quite agreement, but it wasn't argument, either. It hung there, brittle and unresolved, but quieter than anything Mektar would risk answering with.

Finally, Khorlar grunted from his corner. His stoic expression hadn't changed, but his agreement—

or at least his refusal to dissent—carried weight. For now, Zarvash's logic would hold.

Mektar bristled visibly but didn't speak. I didn't bother hiding my satisfaction, letting the faint flicker of a smirk cross my face as I rose to full height. Mektar caught the expression well enough; his sneer returned swiftly.

I left without waiting for his next fumbled insult.

The council chamber's heated tension clung to me as I strode away. Mektar might splutter or rise against Zarvash's surprisingly even logic later, but not tonight. For now, I'd won. Or rather, Zarvash had —his careful threading of caution and reason had defused the worst of it or delayed the inevitable explosion. Mektar's paranoia wasn't extinguished; it was merely smoldering, banked embers waiting for any excuse to blaze.

The path back to the forge was empty. Quiet. A reprieve from the council's festering fear. The tunnels curved ahead, the usual dim lighting casting an even glow across the uneven stone. It should've been a relief to return to solitude.

It wasn't.

The quiet only amplified my thoughts. They tripped over themselves, restless and sharp-edged, leaving trails of unease. The weight of Mektar's accusations mingled with the ache stirred by Selene's presence in the cavern. The momentary distraction of council politics wasn't enough to silence the pull she ignited—not nearly.

Her scent lingered as if she were standing beside me now, that subtle sharp tang of adrenaline threading beneath it. It burned clearly enough in the caverns that it chased me through the tunnels.

I shook my head sharply as I entered the forge, the heat's familiar, oppressive weight closing in fast. It swallowed errant thoughts more effectively than I could. Routine would reset the balance, suppress whatever inconvenient chaos simmered below the surface.

Let it burn out there. Let the heat melt these edges back to something sharp and manageable.

I grabbed a chunk of heat crystal from a supply chest, its grain rough beneath my claws. The chamber was sweltering, hotter than before, but I welcomed it. Anything to sweat out this ridiculous storm in my mind.

It wasn't enough.

The ache that had spread deep within my chest didn't seem to care about logic. It pushed like a simmering pulse against my ribs now, low and insistent. The hammer in my claw was supposed to relieve it. Instead, it dug in further.

I didn't notice I'd started shaping something new

until the clang of metal echoed differently, the sound resonating sharper, crisper than my usual molds. A half-formed blade—a simple design, nothing ornate—formed something rough in my claws.

Selene didn't need weapons. She needed solutions.

But I had none to give.

SIX
SELENE

The cavern was quieter now. The murmur of the sick had stilled, replaced by the hushed voices of Rachel and Kaiya. They were bent low over the wooden table, barely large enough to hold the fragments of gear Orla had pieced together for them. Soft light glinted off Rachel's sweat-streaked hair as she adjusted her makeshift lens, her hands steady as steel. Kaiya hovered beside her, fingers twitching with nervous energy, curiosity radiating like heat from embers.

My gaze flicked between them and the motionless figures of the healers on the other side of the cavern. The air hung thick, metallic with the scent of spilled blood and old herbs.

"Focus the light here," Rachel said, her voice calm despite the tension buried beneath it. She leaned closer to the sample spread thin across a shard of glass. "We need to confirm the structure. If this doesn't match ..."

She let the words trail off. They didn't need finishing. If the medical researcher and xenobiologist couldn't crack this puzzle, it wasn't getting solved.

Kaiya adjusted the light source, her curly hair sticking to her damp forehead. "Got it. There—look. The edges. It's forming those patterns you mentioned." Her voice pitched upward, eager, like she'd forgotten the dead-weight anxiety pressing down on the room.

I stepped closer. "What does that mean?" My voice came out rougher than I meant, but they didn't flinch.

Rachel straightened. Her finger traced the edge of the sample through the lens. "The biochemical structure is consistent with what Mysha described before she passed out. If this plant extract works the way she implied, it should bolster their immune systems and support recovery."

"You're talking about a cure?"

Rachel screwed her face up. "Not exactly. We don't know what's causing the illness. I've been reading Mysha's notes. Or trying to. My Drakarn is still—" She cut herself off. "If anything is going to help, it's this."

"What is it?" They had a vial of dust on their workstation, and there was some kind of paste in a mortar and pestle.

"It's called vyrathis."

Kaiya was wide-eyed. "We've got enough for one dose."

An ache twisted somewhere deep in my chest. I kept my expression steady. "Then we dose Mysha." I stared at the fragment of fluid and crushed leaf spread thin on the glass. The pungent scent of the plant pricked at my nose, sharp and earthy.

It didn't look like salvation. But it felt heavier than anything else in the room.

"How long will it take to see results?" I asked, shifting my weight as I glanced toward the elder's still form, half-buried under blankets.

Rachel exhaled low. "No idea." Her voice stayed calm, but her eyes narrowed in focus as she carefully lifted the sample away and moved toward the small vial beside her. "Are we doing this?"

I let my gaze drag across the cavern again. The sick Drakarn were barely breathing, their scaled chests barely rising. Mysha's form looked small in the wide space. Fragile. It wasn't a word I'd ever associated with the Drakarn before arriving here.

I shoved the thought deep.

"Do it."

Rachel's motions were exact, her hands moving with care honed from years of research in the lab. Kaiya hovered beside her, chewing her lip as she held the light steady.

Mysha was impossibly pale beneath the glow of the heat crystals. Her breathing rasped faintly, like it was dragged from the depths of her chest against her will.

Rachel knelt beside her. "Lift her head, slowly."

I obeyed, gently sliding my hands beneath Mysha's scaled shoulders and cradling her head as Rachel leaned forward with the tube and Kaiya clamped her fingers on either side of Mysha's mouth to make her lips pucker open.

It seemed to sit in her mouth for several seconds before Kaiya stroked her hand down Mysha's throat until she swallowed.

We had to wait.

Mysha's breathing remained shallow, each rasp a reminder of how close she was to slipping away. I let my hands linger beneath her head for a moment longer than necessary, as if holding her steady might anchor her to this world.

No one spoke. Every sound—the shifting of fabric, the bubbling echo of the underground river beyond the far cavern wall, the shallow breaths of the sick—felt amplified in the absence of movement.

Mysha's chest rose and fell weakly.

"Now what?" Kaiya's voice broke the stillness, soft and unsure for a change.

"Now we wait." Rachel straightened from where she crouched. Her hands were shaking slightly, the only crack in her otherwise eerie composure.

Rachel and Kaiya returned to their bench, poring over notes and calculations. I stayed. My eyes were glued to Mysha's face. Her breathing stayed steady now—not stronger, but no worse.

It wasn't much, but it was something, and in the absence of worse news, I'd cling to even the smallest sliver of hope.

The minutes oozed by. Even in my combat days, time had never felt this slow. My muscles were like coiled springs, tension wrung into every inch of me as the acidic thought twisted in my mind —what if this didn't work? What if it was already too late, and we'd held onto hope as only another cruel delusion?

Almost worse, what if it did but we couldn't find more vyrathis to go around?

Mysha shifted, just a bit. Her jaw slackened, lips parting as if her body was remembering it was supposed to breathe. My own breath caught as her claws twitched under my hand.

I scanned her closely. Her chest rose and fell

again—but deeper this time. The rasp clinging to her breath seemed to let go, if only by a fraction.

"Mysha," I whispered, leaning closer like the shift in weight really mattered.

Her head tilted into my touch, and for the first time in days, I swore I saw her scales take on a hint of healthy glow on the edges, faint but unmistakable. Hope kicked in my chest, sharp and sudden.

"She's waking up," I called, voice low but urgent.

Rachel and Kaiya dropped what they were working on and hurried to my side. I hadn't moved, hadn't dared to, as they crouched on either side of Mysha. Rachel's fingers hovered just over Mysha's forehead.

Rachel pressed against the healer's neck. "Heart rate is still weak, but it's not erratic anymore. That's ... good. Very good."

I didn't let go, even as the others hovered, like keeping my hands where they were might hold Mysha together just a little longer. A groan left her throat, soft and strained, and her scaled lips twitched fractionally apart.

"Mysha," I said again, firmer this time, leaning in close enough to catch any change in her breathing, her expression, her still-closed eyes.

Her eyelids fluttered open, just barely, enough

for the glow of the nearby crystals to reflect off her slit-pupil irises. Her gaze darted sluggishly before landing on me. Recognition flickered there, weak but clear.

"Hum ... human," she rasped. Her voice was wrecked, sandpaper and gravel grinding through the single word. But it was hers, and it filled the space like a signal flare in the dark.

"Yeah, it's me," I told her, fighting to keep my voice steady. "You're safe. Rest. Don't try to talk."

She didn't listen, of course. Drakarn never did—not when sheer force of will was basically embedded in their DNA. Her lips worked again, another groan scraping its way out.

Kaiya's hand fluttered toward her own mouth, nerves flooding her expression, but Rachel placed a steadying arm on her shoulder. "Let her speak."

It took several agonizing seconds for Mysha to string something together. Her chest hitched with the effort, muscles jumping beneath her sheer determination. "Rare," she ground out finally, her voice breaking on the single syllable.

I frowned, leaning closer. "What's rare? The illness?"

Her head shifted, a shake side-to-side, and her claws twitched uselessly against the blanket.

"Vyrathis ..." The word came slower, harder, like dragging stone uphill, but its weight dropped between us all the same. "H-har ... Harrovan."

Her strength gave out just as she forced the word through clenched teeth. Her eyes fluttered closed again, but her body had eased in my grip, her breathing leveling out into something quieter—steady, almost peaceful.

Rachel blew out a long breath, tension visibly bleeding from her shoulders. Kaiya leaned back on her heels, clutching her knees, her energy deflating into something closer to numb relief.

"Vyrathis," Rachel repeated. "I'd say that's confirmation we're on the right track."

Kaiya straightened, almost too quickly, her hands shaking with nervous energy again. "But what the hell is Harrovan?"

"That's the next thing we figure out."

I stood, letting my body shift into motion. The ache I'd felt these past days didn't loosen, not fully, but it shifted into something else.

Purpose, maybe.

"You should head back to your quarters and sleep," Kaiya said. "I think Kira said she was going to try and make some bread for us. Rest. You've earned it."

I looked at each of the fifteen unconscious healers and shook my head. "Did either of you sleep last night? At all?"

The doctors shared a guilty look.

"Go sleep. Vega and Terra will be coming in for their shifts soon. There's nothing more you can do right now."

Rachel's eyes were practically black with exhaustion. Kaiya's skin had gone a bit sallow. It didn't take much insisting for them to leave me to it. And, as promised, Vega and Terra showed up.

But I still slept on a little slab in the back of the healing caverns, unwilling to leave my patients.

I ADJUSTED the blanket over Mysha's still form, smoothing it against the cool scales of her chest. Her steady breathing wasn't loud enough to break the silence, but it carved through the oppressive fear clinging to the room. It was quieter in my head now —a small victory.

Mysha was alive, and there was a trail to follow.

The hope sparked by her words hung in the air, tantalizing but incomplete. Harrovan. The word was a puzzle piece in a language I barely understood.

And the weight of what would come next made my fingers twitch with restless energy.

I didn't leave her side. Couldn't bring myself to.

The subtle scrape of claws on stone made my ears prick, and my head turned toward the entrance. Vyne's imposing frame filled the cavern doorway before he ducked to enter fully, his wings folding tighter as he navigated the narrow space. He carried a bundle across his arms, wrapped in thick cloth.

The sight of him sent a strange pulse through my chest, as sharp and sudden as it was unwelcome. My focus snapped back to Mysha, tamping the feeling down as fast as it rose. I didn't have time for *feelings* of any kind.

Vyne's steps were careful, but the air between us shifted as he neared the slab where Mysha rested. His scent again—smoke and something distinctly him—curled into my senses like it belonged there.

"You're back."

"You sound surprised." His voice carried its usual edge of dry disinterest, though it softened slightly. "It's late. Shouldn't you be sleeping?"

"I could ask the same of you." My response was automatic, my eyes still on Mysha's weakly glowing scales. "What's in the bundle?"

He shifted, and the fabric rustled as he set it on the table beside the elder. "More supplies. Forge tools. Salves. Whatever I could gather that might help."

I glanced at the bundle, barely resisting the urge to pick through it. "Good. Thanks."

He huffed once, a sound too soft to be a laugh but still close enough to catch my focus. It made me finally meet his eyes. The dim glow from the crystals caught on the emerald green of his scales, the black diamond-like patterns down his arms and chest marking him like armor.

His gaze didn't waver, though there was something sharper in it. "What happened?"

"Kaiya and Rachel found something that helped Mysha wake up for a bit." The words felt heavier than they should, and for a second I let them hang there, waiting for his reaction. "She gave us a word. Harrovan. She passed out again before we could get anything else."

Vyne's head tilted, his eyes narrowing—not in irritation, but thought. "Harrovan. The mountains."

I blinked. "Mountains?"

"It's a range far east of Scalvaris. The tallest peaks on Volcaryth." His claws tapped once against the stone of the table, the motion measured. "Days away by wing."

Days away. I pressed my lips together, the realization settling uncomfortably. I wasn't sure we had days.

"Someone's going to need to go there," I said after a long breath.

Not me. I couldn't leave. Though my mind flashed briefly to what it might be like to spend a days, a week even, with only Vyne. Heat jolted through me. Even with all the stress of the sickness, a small part of me *wanted* that.

"There's a plant. Vyrathis." The words felt heavy, weighted not just by the distance but what it implied. Logistics, risks, expectations. It wasn't fear—not exactly—but the weight of responsibility wouldn't loosen its grip.

Vyne's eyes stayed on me. They held that same sharpness I'd noticed before, unreadable but somehow too focused, like he could sense the thoughts twisting through my head. "I know it. It's rare."

"And I'm guessing it only grows in the Harrovan mountains?"

His expression didn't shift—no dramatic scoff or flinch, only the tiniest upward quirk of his brow. "Or so I've heard."

"Damn it."

Vyne's wings twitched, a flicker of movement that drew my eyes before I could stop them. He didn't respond, just waited, watching me with that maddeningly calm stare. His presence felt too steady in a moment where everything else frayed at the seams.

"I'll speak with the council," he said. "If you need vyrathis, you'll have it."

SEVEN
VYNE

The council chamber smoldered. Not with fire but with something sharper and far less controlled. Anger. Fear. Weakness masquerading as strength.

Darrokar loomed in the center of the room, the weight of Scalvaris balanced on his shoulders like it was carved there the day he rose to the role of Warrior Lord. His voice bit through the thick tension with the precision of a freshly honed blade.

"It has to be you, Vyne."

I almost laughed, but the flick of my tail was the only visible reaction I allowed. Restraint took effort. "You can't be serious," I said sharply, my voice low but steady. "Send a scouting team. Trained wings accustomed to Harrovan. Not—"

"You." Darrokar's voice cut through every word I hadn't yet said, leaving no cracks for debate. He stepped forward, his wings stretching in a silent warning. "I need someone I can trust. Mektar's causing trouble, and I don't know what in the hells Zarvash is up to. If they put their soldiers on this ..."

My claws curled, dull against the curve of my palms as shadows danced across the blackened stone walls. "Send someone else," I said evenly, though beneath the surface, tension coiled hotter than the nearby forge tunnels. "A group. Resources. You're asking one to accomplish what you need a team to do."

"Two," he corrected.

The room seemed to gather more heat, though perhaps it was just me. A hiss escaped my teeth before I could bury it. "You can't mean one of the humans."

"Yes," Darrokar said simply, his gaze meeting mine without a flicker of doubt or hesitation. It almost made me hate him. "Selene."

Heat crawled beneath my scales. The mere mention of her name made the ache I'd kept chained in the shadows push harder against my ribs. Her scent threaded its way through memory, brighter than the fires in the forge.

I dug my claws into the stone of the table hard enough to leave divots. "She'll die out there."

Darrokar sighed. "She won't. She's resilient. She

was a soldier, just like my Terra. And a medic. She is uniquely suited to this mission."

"Resilient is not immortal," I snapped. "Do you want to give this city another reason to distrust her kind if we fail?"

"She is necessary." Darrokar's words were calm but heavy, clearly chosen with care. "She's been working with the healers for weeks. She knows their ways, their methods. She's already proven her value tenfold. If anyone can identify and handle the vyrathis when it's found, it's her. And I'm sending you with her so you *don't* fail."

"And when the predators out there smell her blood?" My wings shifted, pulling tighter against my back as I spoke.

Darrokar stepped closer, his gaze locking onto mine with that unreadable steel he kept sheathed until moments like this. "Do you doubt me so much, Vyne?"

The air thickened between us. My tail flicked, carving a line through the heated silence. "I don't doubt you," I said finally. "I doubt the wisdom of this."

Darrokar tilted his head, the movement as deliberate as every measured step he'd taken until now. "Do you?"

I hated how clearly he could see through me.

Beneath my objections, my resistance, the truth pulsed too close to the surface: It wasn't just the danger of the Harrovan mountains that made my chest tighten with every second of this discussion. It was her. Selene. The thought of spending days—and nights—alone with her, her scent driving every instinct to places I couldn't afford to go. I doubted myself more than I did the world beyond Scalvaris.

But some truths wouldn't be spoken here. Darrokar didn't press further, though his gaze stayed sharp.

"I trust you," he said instead, his tone deceptively simple. "So will you trust me?"

"Trust doesn't make mountains less deadly."

"And doubt weakens resolve," he countered, his arms crossing over his broad chest. "Which will you carry into this mission?"

I closed my fist against the stone table, letting the heat seep deep into the muscles of my arm before I finally forced the words from my throat. "Fine."

Darrokar gave a single nod, one that somehow carried more weight than the anvil in my forge.

"Good," he said simply. "You leave at dawn. Report to Selene tonight and ensure she has what she needs. I'm trusting you with this."

I didn't respond beyond the sharp lash of my tail

against the stone as I turned toward the chamber's exit.

As I stalked into the tunnels, the heat of the council chamber faded behind me. But the ache in my chest—sharp, heavy, and distinctly hers—burned hotter still.

THE AIR outside the healing caverns clung to me like ash settling over scorched earth. This small alcove, cut into the outer wall of the tunnels, was a place meant for reprieve—a moment of peace amid chaos. The world here didn't burn; it breathed. Quiet. Cool. Patient.

And yet, the tension in my chest pulled taut as I took in the figure sitting against the ledge.

Selene.

She was curled in on herself in the way someone does when fighting sleep too long, her legs drawn up, arms hooked loosely around her knees. Her dark hair, usually pulled back tight like she was braced for battle, hung limp in loose waves over her shoulders.

The lines of her posture screamed weariness, but her eyes, locked on some unseen point in the dim haze beyond, glinted with a determination I doubted even her own body could quench. Shadowed though they were above the pale hollows of her cheeks, they burned, defying everything around her, even herself.

Her head tilted, her shoulders stiffening an infinitesimal amount. It wasn't defiance, just awareness. Preemptive defense, perhaps. This woman was carved of sharp edges and blunt truths.

"What are you doing here?" she murmured. Her voice was low, roughened at the edges, yet calm. Steady. Like someone who wasn't surprised anymore by disappointment circling back for another hit. "Come to give more bad news?"

The bitter edge under her tone cracked something in my chest I hadn't realized was fragile in the first place.

"I come with orders," I said, stepping fully into the meager light.

Her lip quirked, the shadow of that sharp humor pressing through exhaustion. "Figures."

Her head peeked to the side, sparing me a glance cut from steel and smoothed by something too soft for either of us to name. Whatever she was bracing for—criticism, dismissal, more endless pressure—it sat coiled behind that glance, an invisible wall built brick by goddamn stubborn brick.

I lowered myself to the stone beside her without asking. My tail curled once, instinctively tucking to the side so it wouldn't crowd her space. Selene shifted, not away but inward, crossing her arms like she had to build another barrier between herself and whatever weight she'd been forced to carry all day.

I waited. She would speak when she wanted to and not a moment before.

It didn't take long.

"One of them died." Voice flat. Heavy. Not cracked or broken, but brittle, like glass about to shatter under its own strain.

Every muscle in my body stiffened. "Who?"

"A young one. Yaris." She exhaled hard, fingers dragging briefly through her hair before falling limply at her sides again. "He wasn't ... he wasn't doing well by the time we got to him, but I thought—I thought maybe ..." Her voice trailed off, unfinished, swallowed by the vast emptiness carried in her too-quiet breath.

She shook her head sharply, but not to erase what she'd said. Just to shove it somewhere else, some dark corner she wasn't going to look at long enough to let it sink fully in.

"Barely old enough to be here," she muttered, quieter now but no less sharp. "He had this laugh. Quick and stupid and bright—damn near drove Kaiya insane this past week." Her lips twisted, as if memory could still find humor in agony. "Then he just ... stopped."

Guilt flashed across her eyes. The kind that left scars deeper than any blade could carve. I knew the weight well; it lived in my own chest some nights with wounds I'd long since buried.

"You did what you could."

She barked a laugh—not cruel, not humorless, but something sharp and self-deprecating. Her head tilted down briefly. "I couldn't do shit."

The air tightened around us—not choking, but charged. I wanted to reach out, to tug that weight from her shoulders and crush it under my claws before it swallowed her whole. But my hands stayed where they were, clenched against my knees. Her scent was sharp in the stillness, krysfruit wrapping around the ember-smoke of grief laced in her skin. Everything about her pulled against the ache in my chest I'd tried—and failed—to quench since the first time I'd met her.

I should have left. Should've delivered my orders and gone to deal with the rest of the mission's logistics. But the thought of walking away while Yaris's shadow still lingered in her expression made my claws curl hard enough to bite into my own palms.

"He wasn't on you," I said finally, my voice low enough it barely carried across the space between us. "None of this is."

She didn't look at me. But her lips pressed into a

tight line as her hands curled at her sides, nails dragging against the fabric of her pants.

"Harrovan." My voice shifted deliberately, the
single name slicing into the quiet between us, though
the tension in it made my stomach twist.

That made her finally look at me. "What?"

"That's where we're going." The words left me
heavy as the stone beneath us. "Darrokar ordered it.
You and I leave at dawn."

Her reaction wasn't what I expected. Not anger
or frustration. Not even the exhaustion driving
everything else. It was just stillness. Like she hadn't
registered the words yet. Like her mind was playing
catch-up with her defenses.

Her lips parted once, then snapped shut. She
shook her head, faint and definite. "No."

I blinked. "No?"

"I mean no. As in, not happening. As in, my
place is here," she said, steel sparking through the
weariness clogging her voice. "You can't just ... Hell
no. I'm not leaving the healers now. They need me."

"They need you to retrieve the cure."

Her frame stiffened, her arms raising to cross
tightly over her chest as though bracing against me—
or perhaps herself. "They need me now."

"They'll need you more if they're still alive when
we return."

The response silenced her, but her eyes cut dangerously toward mine, a flicker of heat beneath both her defiance and grief. "You're so sure we can even find it?"

"Yes." I meant it, even though the rough trek through Harrovan clawed over my mind like a poorly woven net. Her mortality against its dangers would haunt me every step beyond the city's barriers, but here, now, watching her try to climb a wall made of her own stubborn will and bruised instincts—I wouldn't let her crumble only to chain herself to failure's corpse.

Selene's jaw twitched, tension tracing her frame as she exhaled sharply through her nose. "You've been up there, then? Harrovan?"

"No." My tone stayed steady; it softened only where her shoulders stiffened further. "But I'll make sure you're not left to face it alone."

Her lips almost curled into a smile before her eyes dropped again, low and far away from the dim blue glow of the river.

The silence pressed down again, heavy but not the same weight as before. It shifted too much, too soon. Too clear. Above the grief thick in the air, something else edged closer, closer to the space we'd left untouched since the moment we first crossed paths.

I crossed it before I could think better of it.

My hand moved first—not grabbing, not holding, but hovering above her shoulder as my wings shifted open, slow, deliberate. The tip of my left one curled toward her back, brushing her upper spine like a shield offering itself where words would always fail. "Let me give you strength," I murmured, my voice low and rough-edged against the quiet.

She didn't jerk away. Didn't move at all, in fact, as my claws hovered against her, hesitant to thunder through whatever fragile thread she was clinging to here in this little alcove. After too many suspended heartbeats, her body softened, muscles easing toward the contact.

Her voice barely breached the quiet, but when it did, it refused to waver. "Just for a little while."

Something in me cracked wide open. It wasn't a break, not really, but a fracture deeper than I cared to name. As her weight shifted just slightly against my wing, I felt her warmth leeching through the fragile space we'd allowed between us.

I let it happen.

The world around us drew quiet, as if Volcaryth itself had decided to hold its breath. Her exhaustion had a gravity of its own, pulling everything close into its orbit, me included.

Her hair brushed against the curve of my wing,

barely a whisper, but even that little touch sent my instincts reeling. Every sinew of restraint I held threatened to fray as her scent wrapped around me—smoke, krysfruit, and something sharper, tinged with sadness.

I exhaled through my nose, steady and slow, while my claws curled against the stone beneath us. "We will make it back," I said, breaking the stillness between us. My voice was rougher than I intended, lower, but steady. "To the healers. To this place. I won't fail you."

Her head tilted, her cheek brushing the edge of my wing, whether consciously or not I couldn't tell. She let out a soft, humorless laugh, the kind that didn't belong to someone who fully believed what they'd just heard. "And what if we do?"

Her question wasn't meant to challenge. It wasn't defiant. It was quiet and jagged around the edges like a blade that hadn't been polished properly.

"You and I don't fail." I said it again, slower this time, stronger, hoping she could pull the weight of those words into her chest and carry them with the same intensity I felt.

Selene raised her head just enough to glance at me. The shadows of her exhaustion and stubbornness waged war in her eyes, dark and cutting but too human for her to conceal entirely. For a moment, I could see the soldier in her fighting the medic. The part of her that wanted to move forward, to push and charge and fix, battling the part that had known loss and carried it far longer than anyone deserved.

"That easy, huh?" she said, the faintest flicker of dry humor threading her voice. "Why don't you package that up for the rest of us mortals?"

I snorted softly—the sound rough and unpolished even to my own ears. "Mortals?" I echoed, the word rolling over my tongue like there'd been a joke buried in it once. "Hard to believe you think of yourself that way."

Her brow quirked, a spark of something sharper flashing in her tired gaze. "Oh, don't worry. You Drakarn don't let us humans forget where we fall on the food chain." The corners of her mouth twitched upward, though not quite into the shape of a smile.

That humor was enough to kindle something warmer, brighter than the ache underneath. It was enough to anchor me against the instinct clawing beneath my scales.

"Harrovan isn't the food chain you need to worry about," I said, though my tone stayed lighter than the words themselves. "But if it helps, I'll make sure any predators out there know exactly where they fall."

Her lips tugged upward a little more, though the

weariness in her expression still weighed her features down. "Big talk."

I leaned back, letting the tilt of my wings shift just so, not enough to pull away but enough to cut the sharp edges of what still lingered between us. "Big claws."

That earned a small laugh—real but wry, edged with disbelief but unharmed by it. She shook her head but leaned forward again, her breath soft and even as she stared past me.

For a while, neither of us said anything.

Her scent lingered in the alcove, threading through the cool air like a constant reminder of things I had no right to think about. The warmth of her shoulder, so close to brushing mine—and the quiver of her resolve beneath it—snared my focus in a way I hated but couldn't seem to shake.

No predator worth its fangs ignored what was right in front of them, but this was something else entirely.

I shifted against the stone. The scrape of my claws filled the silence, breaking it just enough without fracturing the fragile calm that had settled. "We leave at dawn," I reminded her, my tone softer, less edged now. "Get some rest."

Selene turned her head a little, her dark eyes cutting upward to meet mine. There was no sharpness in her stare this time—no challenge, no defiance. Just tired steel. And beneath it, something that flickered too faintly to trust the shape of. "Easy for you to say," she murmured, her lips curling in a sardonic edge. "Pretty sure you Drakarn can fall asleep standing upright."

I huffed, a sound small and guttural in the back of my throat. "We can. But you're not Drakarn."

"No kidding," she said wryly, pressing her palms into her knees as if preparing to rise. Her glance dropped, and the shadows along her face deepened under the quiet glow of the river's light. "But seriously—look at me. You think I'm just going to flip myself 'off' after this?"

I tilted my head, my wings giving the slightest flick of acknowledgment. "You need to try." My voice lowered further, rough and honest. "Exhaustion gets you killed. Especially where we're going."

Her lips parted, argument at the ready. But her words caught somewhere between her mind and her mouth, and what finally escaped wasn't anger or sarcasm, just a long, quiet exhale. She leaned forward, bracing her elbows on her knees, and dragged a tired hand through her hair. "You think I haven't been trying?"

I made no reply. None was required. The

rawness in her voice—quiet as it was—said more than anything I could offer.

The silence stretched between us, softer this time. Not heavy, just steady. Long minutes passed, or maybe only seconds. I didn't count. I just stayed still, watching her from the corner of my eye while the ache buried beneath my ribs pressed harder with each passing breath.

Finally, Selene rose to her feet, the motion practiced but stiff. The fatigue etched in her posture caught the glow of the distant light, shadow and glow playing against her every step. She turned just enough to glance over her shoulder, one hand resting on her hip as her other reached up to tuck a stray strand of hair behind her ear.

"So," she drawled lightly, the humor barely masking the honesty beneath it, "dawn, huh?"

I smirked—a flicker of warmth that betrayed more than I cared to admit. "At dawn."

Her brows quirked in response, her lips tilting upward in a humorless smile. She held my gaze just a moment longer before looking away, her jaw tightening as she shifted her weight on her heels.

"Don't be late." Her words were almost teasing, as though speaking them aloud lightened the atmosphere just enough to make it tolerable again.

"I'll be waiting."

EIGHT
VYNE

Pre-dawn was quiet in Scalvaris. Time blurred under the rock, the suns just a hint through the skyshafts that pierced the ceiling of our city.

The air was heavy. Tense. And in that quiet stillness, I could feel the city bracing for the threat creeping ever closer to its borders. It was more than the sickness festering in the healers' caverns. It was something larger—something clawing at the edges of Scalvaris, unseen and unspoken.

The weight pressing against my chest wasn't the city's fear. It was something sharper.

Selene.

Krysfruit. Smoke.

It tickled my nose before I heard her footsteps.

She emerged from the edge of the quarter, her figure cutting a sharp line against the glow spilling over the stones. Her hair was tied back, though already some loose strands curled and stuck against her skin. The strength of her frame—the set of her shoulders, the weight in her step—didn't waver, but something else clung to her.

Weariness. Hesitation. Quiet grief behind a mask of sharp focus.

My tongue—traitorous, damnable thing—tingled at the edges, a phantom sensation I couldn't banish no matter how tightly I locked my jaw.

When our eyes finally locked, it hit harder than I anticipated. She stiffened for just a moment, a flicker of something unguarded before those dark eyes leveled me.

"Not too many early risers in Scalvaris?" Her voice was even, carefully controlled, though the faint humor threaded in it betrayed her efforts.

I forced a wry smirk, though the weight in my chest didn't loosen. "You're late."

"Am I?" I could see the ghost of a smile tugging the corner of her lips as she stepped closer. "You could have left without me."

"You must be lucky."

Her expression sobered, the humor retreating back into the quiet defenses she always carried. "Lucky's not exactly what I've been lately."

The words weren't sharp enough to cut, but they

landed heavier than a mere observation. They sat awkwardly in the space between us, refusing to be smoothed over or walked around.

I tuned my senses back to the mission, letting practicality sand down the edges of everything else. "We'll make our way through the tunnels first, then out to the peaks." My wings shifted, the scrape of my claws mimicking the restless twitch in my shoulders. "We'll stop where we can find shelter come midday."

Her chin dipped, a small, fractional motion that said enough. Her fingers fiddled with the straps of her pack as she adjusted its position with combat trained precision.

Her motions were steady and calm as I studied her. She'd been a soldier once, and it showed. I shouldn't have cared beyond how it would help the mission. I shouldn't have noticed. But every inch of her stole my focus anyway.

Her scent. The set of her jaw. The stubborn line of determination cutting through exhaustion in her eyes.

Gods above, she was— No. Stop.

I forced myself to glance away, my gaze sweeping over the morning glow of the river instead. "Ready?"

Selene huffed softly and adjusted her pack again. "Lead the way."

Her voice might have been steady. Her steps

resolute. But as we moved toward the tunnels carved into the cavern wall, that same weight coiled tighter with every step. It clung to the silence between us, unspoken but impossible to ignore, no matter how far we went.

I could hear her breathe. Too clear in the tunnels. Too close. The soft rhythm of it was steady, to her credit—controlled despite the strain of exhaustion I knew ate at her body and mind. Her pack jostled against her back, the sound blending with the quiet scrape of her boot against stone.

She brushed against me, her arm, her shoulder, maybe both, catching against the tough curve of my own as the path narrowed to little more than a cramped corridor. The contact was light, but the spark it sent through my nerves lingered. Heat prickled along the ridge of my spine. I forced my wings tighter along my back, trying to reclaim the space between us, but there wasn't any.

Selene stepped back to compensate, muttering, "Bit tight in here, huh?"

Her voice was low in the winding echoes of the tunnel. But the way it cut through the silence between us was sharp enough to draw my attention.

"Only for those who aren't paying attention." My voice was as dry as I could make it. A reflex. A defense.

She gave me a narrow look, though the faintest twist of amusement tugged her lips upward. "Of course. Because your wings don't seem to be taking up half the path."

"They're efficient. Unlike your stride."

She let out a sharp breath just this side of laughter. Her pace didn't falter, and when her shoulder brushed mine again, this time she didn't pull back so quickly. I didn't think it was on purpose, but the contact lingered.

My claws flexed against the rock for balance, the scrape unnervingly loud in the too-close air. Her scent was even stronger now, distinct and maddening. My tongue tingled again, that same cursed sensitivity pulling my focus where it didn't belong.

We crossed a sudden dip in the floor—a pocket of uneven stone that split the path where magma had once scorched through centuries prior. It forced her step to falter, her footing catching awkwardly, though she masked it quickly and pressed forward. I caught her movement before my mind registered what I was doing, my wing shifting instinctively to steady her balance.

Her hand shot out, reflexive. It wasn't enough to grab me—she didn't—and instead her fingers caught the edge of the wall beside her.

"Careful," I muttered before I could stop myself.

Her head tilted, sharp and questioning, though her pace didn't falter again. "I've got it."

Her dark eyes cut toward me as much as the tunnel allowed, the shadows obscuring the finer details of her expression but not enough to dim the glint of teasing steel in her gaze.

"Is there a reason we're not flying? Or are those wings of yours just for show?"

I bristled, wings flaring, sharp taloned tips scraping against the narrow cave wall. "The path to the Harrovan Mountains would take us too close to a field of noxious gas given off by one of the volcanoes. If we leave by the entrance at the end of this path, we'll avoid it. And keep breathing."

"Breathing is the preferable option."

The tunnel opened after a sharp bend, giving us a bit more room to breathe. Selene exhaled low, like she'd been carrying the weight deep inside her and could finally draw a full breath.

I glanced over at her. A scar ran along her temple, thin but sharp enough to suggest violence, caught the light as she turned and something dangerously close to *need* clenched in my chest.

"That scar. Is it from fighting for them?" I asked quietly, the words slipping before I could rationalize the cost of asking.

Selene paused, her brow tightening in confusion. "Them?"

"The humans. Whatever you call them. Your warriors."

She didn't speak immediately. Her fingers brushed against her temple, tracing the old wound. Finally, she rolled one shoulder in a small shrug, though the motion looked heavier than it should have. "No, my scar didn't come from battle. A piece of glass hit me when I was fourteen. From a broken bottle. Wrong place, wrong time sort of thing. I joined the army for the usual reason: college."

My jaw tensed, muscles pulling tight in my throat though I wasn't sure why. "I don't understand." What was *college?* She spoke Drakarn now, thanks to some little piece of Earth technology, but the word didn't translate.

"School," she said, and this time I knew the word. "I was supposed to serve out my contract and then they'd pay for my education. Then my superiors offered another option. I could leave early if I volunteered to go on the generation ship. They needed more medical professionals. I'm not a doctor or anything, but I was promised more education. More room for advancement. And it wasn't like there was a life I was missing out on at home. I'm not like Kira; I'm not missing a sister or anything like that. I thought this would be the opportunity of a lifetime."

"And instead you ended up here."

"This was definitely not what I was promised." She cast a sidelong glance my way. "But it's not all bad."

Her scent burned sharper against the compact air, and I swore the space had grown smaller again, closer. Too close.

When I spoke, my voice came quieter, rougher at the edges. "Good."

"What about you?" she tossed the words out casually, probing but not prying. "How did you become a forge master?"

"I forged my first blade when I was eight," I said. "It wasn't sharp, but I liked the shape. My father liked the ambition. That was enough."

Her expression flickered—soft, if only slightly. "Eight. Damn."

Selene's steps faltered briefly, her boot snagging over an irregular break in the rock, and for a moment, her weight pitched forward. My arm shot out before my brain caught up, steadying her without finesse until she was flattened against my chest.

I let her go quickly, but it was useless. The tunnel narrowed again, forcing her step closer to mine. As her arm brushed mine for the second time, any rational thought left unraveled, fraying at the edges faster than I could hide it.

Her scent burned sharper now. It wrapped around me in the confines of the tunnel, teasing the fragile chain of control I'd forced around my instincts since the moment I'd first tasted the air near her.

For the forge's sake.

My gaze dropped briefly, catching the subtle shift of her shoulders—the sharp cut of bone against her skin, her frame wound just tightly enough that I could feel her bracing for something invisible but inescapable. She wore her strength like armor, too heavy in some places, but almost too worn near others. And it only made the ache inside me twist deeper.

Damn it all.

I fixed my stare forward again, unwilling to crumble under the instinct clawing against sense. There wasn't space here—not now, not in this tunnel, not anywhere between us for what my body sought so painfully.

The tunnel's oppressive grip finally began to loosen as light from the end—faint and pale, but unmistakable—glimmered ahead. My steps slowed.

Selene caught my hesitation, her own movements faltering briefly before she drew up alongside me. Her breathing was quieter now, steadier, though her stance remained sharp-edged, like she was bracing for whatever lay just beyond our line of sight.

She stepped forward, her boot scratching against the stone as she moved closer to the growing glow. The dim warmth of the rising suns had started to bleed into the cool blue hue of the crystals, casting flickering shadows that danced along the rough walls. The air felt lighter here, cooler, though brimming with a strange tension that hummed beneath the surface like unseen currents.

I moved up beside her, wings rustling as they adjusted to the wider space. I took a moment to savor the more open space, but only for a moment. I didn't want her to think I was hesitating.

Selene looked out over the distant horizon. Quiet tension radiated off her. "It's beautiful," she said softly, almost as though the words weren't meant for me to hear.

"It's beautiful, but it burns," I responded. Even with my scales, the surface of Volcaryth was unkind.

She didn't look at me. "I figured as much."

The steep drop from the tunnel mouth to the terrain below yawned open just steps away. The winds swirled through the air, teasing the edges of my wings.

"You're not afraid of heights," I said, more statement than question. Her steady stance told me as much.

"No." Her response was clipped, matter-of-fact. But she still glanced at the distance below with a narrowed gaze. "But that doesn't mean I'm not cautious. It's not like I have wings."

"That's why you have me."

She blinked, finally turning toward me. Her lips curved, though the humor in her smile didn't quite reach her eyes. "Are you always this reassuring?"

"Only when it's warranted."

"Lucky me." Her tone softened, faint amusement lacing her exhaustion.

I stepped closer. The rock beneath my feet shifted, but I ignored it, wings flaring as I gestured toward the open sky beyond the ledge.

"Get closer," I said, my voice cool, though something in my chest twisted as her gaze flicked toward me with an oddly suspicious arch of her brow.

Her jaw tensed, but she didn't argue. Instead, she inhaled sharply through her nose, muttering something under her breath that sounded like either a curse or a prayer. Then she stepped closer to the edge of the tunnel. Her frame was still as strong as ever, but I caught the flicker of hesitation in her stance as she glanced one last time at the drop awaiting her.

I opened my wings fully, the stretch of them casting shifting shadows that sliced across the rock at our feet. The motion forced her step closer, keeping her within reach. I extended an arm, my claws flexing briefly before curling tightly against the leather guard at my wrist.

"Don't flinch."

Her eyes narrowed. "What—?"

Before she could finish, my arm circled firmly around her waist. It wasn't rough—precisely measured, controlled, but undeniably close. I pulled her against me as my other arm moved to steady her back, claws grazing just briefly against the strap of her pack. My wings closed, angling around her frame without fully enveloping her. Not yet. I wrapped my tail around her legs to keep her as close as possible.

Selene stiffened, her breath catching at the contact. Her hands instinctively shot to the front of my armor, gripping the edges of the leather as her stance fought against faltering completely.

"This is practical," I offered, though my voice was rougher than intended. She didn't need to know how much it cost me to keep my control. "For both our sakes."

She didn't respond immediately. Her gaze flicked toward the open sky behind me, her hands still gripping the edge of my worn leathers like she was weighing every possible escape plan.

"Right," she said finally, though the edge of her voice gave away her own internal battle. "Practical."

Stars help me.

That close, every sense I had was on fire—her breath warm against my throat, the heat of her skin radiating through the armor and scales separating us. My claws itched for purchase they couldn't take, my wings shifting instinctively to tighten around her, shielding her fully within their span as the wind curled tighter around us.

"Ready?" I asked, my voice softened by a restraint that grated against everything primal inside me.

She nodded once, her grip tightening. "Don't drop me."

The faintest twitch curled at the corner of my lips—a bitter, aching smile rising to fight the storm raging beneath the rest of me. "Not a chance."

NINE
SELENE

The wind hammered at my face, sending a wild snarl through my hair and a hot spike of terror through my stomach. My arms tightened around Vyne's neck—not because I didn't trust him, but because trust wasn't about to overrule every screaming survival instinct raging in my chest.

The ground plummeted away beneath us like it hated me personally, and for one long, dizzying second, I swallowed the sharp, indignant protest of a species that had never been meant to leave the ground.

Vyne's hold didn't falter. One arm braced across my back, the other curved beneath my thighs, anchoring me against the unshakeable heat and strength of him as his wings unfolded and snapped open with merciless precision. The sheer size of them—dark, rippling planes of muscle and membrane stretching impossibly wide—made the clipped edge of awe lurking beneath my anxiety harder to shove down than I liked.

I was trying not to think about the tail wrapped around my legs. Judging from the blushes I'd seen from both Terra and Orla, Drakarn could be wickedly precise with their tails.

Volcaryth unfurled beneath us, a hellscape alive with fire and stone and smoke. Crimson sands twisted into blackened cliffs, their jagged spines punctuated by menacing veins of rivers that glowed molten-bright against the scorched ground. Steam hissed from unseen rifts below, curling up into the shimmering waves of heat that distorted everything into a feverish haze. The air cut sharp and sour in my throat, tinged with sulfur so thick it clung to the back of my tongue no matter how carefully I breathed.

It was hell. And somehow … it was beautiful.

I glanced down, curiosity overriding my better judgement for half a second. Mistake. My stomach flipped violently as I registered how far we already were from the tunnels of Scalvaris. The cliffs were tiny teeth now, sharp and impossibly far away. I squeezed my eyes shut before the lurch in my stomach could claw its way up to my throat.

"You sure you've got me?" The words escaped

before I could think about stopping them. I tried to make the question sound teasing, but it came out tighter than I liked.

Vyne's voice cut through the chaotic wind, rough around the edges but maddeningly calm. His tone held no sense of strain despite the sheer size and weight of me that he carried as easily as breathing. "Do you think I'd bring you this far just to drop you?"

It was the dry precision in his words—not teasing, but not quite cutting—that had me snorting despite myself. "No."

His wings adjusted, catching a rising thermal draft with an expert, calculated shift that had the cruel audacity to make me feel momentarily weightless.

Without meaning to, I was noticing things about him again. Details I didn't want to focus on, like the ripple of his muscles beneath my legs and the press of heat through the smooth hardness of his scaled skin where it touched mine. Even his scent beneath the sulfuric sting of Volcaryth was distractingly, infuriatingly distinct—something rich and scorched and impossible to name.

It was too much. Too close.

My jaw clenched against the strange coil of unease threading low in me, and I resettled my grip on him like that would do something. His heat washed over me, unrelenting even against the hot currents of air buffeting us higher.

"You can relax," he said. His voice dipped into something low and firm. "You're safer in my arms than you would be on the ground."

"Tell that to gravity," I retorted, though not even sarcasm could steady my voice.

His wings snapped outward in a subtle tilt that sent us gliding on a slower descent now, the currents catching waves to lift us against the searing sky. "Humans need to adapt if they want to survive here," he replied, the blunt, matter-of-fact cadence of his words landing heavier than they needed to.

I aimed a sharp glance upward at him, my lips twitching despite myself. "Wow. Thanks for that astute insight."

He didn't respond. But there was something almost deliberate in the flicker of his wings again as he settled further into the air current, arms shifting at my waist like the motion was every bit as natural to him as breathing.

By the time his wings cut into a sharper angle upward again, I could feel the strength in his frame flexing with every shift of the flight. It was natural, fluid in a way that couldn't quite be called effort. His focus was sharp and unnerving, but there was never hesitation. Not in the way he moved. Not in the way he latched his hand tighter at the closest pull of hot wind, his claws brushing just barely against my skin.

The world blurred below, marked by endless fractured spines of rock glowing faint with the veins of lava that scoured the surface. The heat pushed harder and harder against my body with every fucking mile. And I hated it—hated the way I could feel the rhythm of his wings aligning quietly with the pounding pulse in my ears, hated the strange steadiness it offered when my instincts wanted chaos.

I sighed. "Is it always this goddamn hot?"

"It can freeze at night," Vyne responded, his clipped reply carrying just enough authority to kill any expectation of sugarcoating.

"Hell of a tourism ad."

One wing shifted just slightly, setting the wind curling close enough to rattle the strands of hair clinging to sweat at the side of my face. "We don't get many tourists."

A hot wind slammed against us, fierce with its timing. His grip tightened briefly, just enough to keep me steady as he adjusted in a single motion. That seamless control—sharp and effortless, even as the gust clawed at us—set something coiling low in my stomach. I ignored it. Tried to. But it lingered, sparking against frayed nerves and tuning me too closely to the heat of his body pressed to mine.

We flew on like that, stretched tight between the hovering nowheres of earth and sky. The weight of his closeness grated against my already shredded composure, impossible to shake. By the time the broken peaks of volcanic cliffs rose beneath us, cracks against the sky, my muscles felt stitched together with something fragile and thin.

"Hold on," Vyne said, his voice cutting through the thick air.

Instinct tightened my arms around him. Before I had the chance to second-guess, his wings folded in, angling us into a dive so sharp it seemed to pull the breath right from my chest. The wind churned around us, violent and hot, testing his control, but his hold didn't falter—not once. Just before we hit the outcrop where rock jutted out from the cliffs, his wings snapped open. The force of it caught us, slowing us just enough for what should've been a smooth landing.

For him, at least.

My knees immediately tried to quit on me the moment my boots hit the ground. Adrenaline licked through me in waves, raw and unsteady, but his hand stayed firm on my arm, keeping me upright until I finally found my balance. Blood pounded in my ears, tangled up with the burn in my chest and the heat soaking into my skin. When he let go, slowly, it was almost too careful. Like he wasn't sure if I'd crumple or not.

I didn't. Not physically, at least.

A breath rattled through me, but it scraped too harsh, nearly sticking to the thick heat swallowing the plateau like a second atmosphere. My hands drifted to my knees as I leaned just far enough to keep the vertigo at bay.

"That," I said between gulps of air, my voice cracking at the edges, "was objectively terrifying."

A low sound escaped him—not quite a laugh, but close enough to knock my focus off-center. "You held up better than I expected."

"You're lucky I didn't ..." I trailed off. No way I was about to admit I'd been five seconds away from losing my lunch all over his armor. "Forget it."

Vyne's gaze lingered, heavy enough that I didn't need to look up to feel it. It was the silence that got me more than anything—the weight of what wasn't being said. Loud and crushing, louder than any words ever could've been. I straightened, swallowing hard against the dryness clawing at my throat.

A shadow flickered in my periphery, and I turned to see him holding out a small canteen. Its surface gleamed against the distorted light—dented and scuffed, as though it had survived more miles of this harsh terrain than I had any hope of matching.

I hesitated, just briefly.

Then I reached for it.

Our fingers brushed.

The contact was so small, barely enough to count, but it sparked through the noise of everything else. The heat of his hand—too warm, somehow even hotter than the blasted air around us—touched the clammy bite of mine, and something inside me jolted. My spine stiffened, my lungs turned traitor, choking my breath into a brief, stuttering hitch before letting go again.

He flinched first.

Just barely, but it was there. The canteen passed into my hand, but his fingers pulled back like he'd touched live flames. A sharp, gruff sound slipped from him, as if he'd meant to smother the reaction but hadn't quite managed to rein it in. His wings twitched, a tension barely breaking through before snapping back under tight control.

I looked down, pretending I hadn't noticed. Pretending my hands were busy with something as ordinary as unscrewing the cap of the canteen and not still trembling.

"Thanks," I said, my voice scraping against the dryness in my throat as I uncapped the canteen. I focused wholly on the cool stream of water sliding past the harsh burn of the sulfur-thick air. For a moment, it was the only relief in the oppressive heat pressing on every part of me, carving its way through the metallic taste left there by Volcaryth's unrelenting assault.

Capping the canteen, I tossed it in his direction —not out of recklessness, exactly, but out of some base-level frustration that had hitched itself to my nerves and refused to let go. Vyne caught it so cleanly he might as well have anticipated my motion, his claws folding around the dented metal without a word.

"Rest." The command was impassive, his focus barely darting toward me before it turned to survey the ridge surrounding us. "We'll camp here for the night."

"You don't have to tell me twice," I said, retreating to a wide, flat rock hugged tight to the plateau's central ridge. The surface burned against my skin when I perched on it, but I sank into the contact anyway, resisting the urge to lean back fully for fear my shirt might melt into the stone.

Vyne moved with sharp efficiency, every step precise. His tail snaked behind him, shifting grains of stony grit as he crossed the edge of the plateau to comb its perimeter. His body remained taut with focus, though nothing about it telegraphed alarm. It was a rhythm of constant readiness, practiced and almost predatorially smooth—the kind of presence that demanded awareness even when it didn't actively threaten.

I hated that he drew my focus the way he did. His movement, the way the dark gleam of his scaled form swallowed every trickle of heat shimmering between the molten landscape below and the rock pressing beneath me. With each measured turn, his arms adjusted their balance against his armor, claws flexing—not in unease but in idle control, as if each sharpened edge had been designed down to its smallest detail for lethal purpose.

He wasn't handsome, not really. That word was for softer things. Safer things.

What Vyne was ... it didn't fit into anything soft or safe.

And that dip in my stomach as my gaze moved along his line another fraction farther?

Definitely the heat.

DARKNESS DESCENDED on Volcaryth in a slow, simmering fade, turning the molten glow of the landscape into something ember lit. Even the heat withdrew, leaving a sharp breeze behind. I huddled against a wedge of stone, arms wrapped around my knees, trying to ignore the clammy cling of my sweat-drenched clothes.

Vyne settled across from me, rummaging through the pack by his side. Weariness seeped into my bones after the day's flight, but it was the gnawing anxiety over the healers that kept me restless. I watched him produce a few strips of dried meat, and my stomach knotted. When he offered one, I accepted, chewing carefully.

His tail drifted in a lazy arc behind him, but there was nothing lazy about his vigilance as he scanned the sky every so often for threats. Even so, he placed a canteen of water beside me with a gentle motion. For a moment I resented that kindness, how it stirred a raw, unfamiliar ache.

"You're worried," Vyne said at last.

No shit. I swallowed the dry hunk of meat, trying to gather my thoughts. "The healers—the sickness." My throat tightened, forcing me to reach for the water. "I keep picturing them, waiting ... running out of time."

His eyes searched mine. "We'll find this blasted plant," he said. "They'll hold on until then."

"You can't know that," I whispered. Fear and guilt twisted in my chest.

Vyne exhaled, his tail brushing once against the stone before it fell still. "What use is it to fear otherwise? Now eat." He handed me another strip of meat.

I forced it down.

Later, Vyne beckoned me toward a slab of rock that formed a partial windbreak. I glanced at the sky's bruised purple glow, night swallowing the last thread of daylight.

"You should get some sleep."

The dropping temperature made me shiver even harder, and I wrapped a cloak around my shoulders and settled in, my knees pulled tight against my chest as the wind hissed over the ridge. My mind felt too loud for sleep, every half-formed worry fixating on Scalvaris and its ailing patients.

Time slipped.

It could have been minutes or hours of half-dream, half-wake, when the rustle of wings startled me. Vyne knelt close, his face caught in shifting shadows, the draconic lines seeming even more alien in the faint light.

"You're trembling," he said. "Are you cold?"

"I'm okay," I muttered, but I couldn't hide the way my teeth were practically chattering.

"Suffering will do neither of us any good." He hesitated, then extended one wing around my side.

The great, leathery span shut out the wind and was almost shockingly warm.

A ripple of heat spread through me. I breathed in, trying to collect my wits as the sudden contrast— bitter cold on one side, radiant heat on the other— made my awareness spike. Who was I kidding? Awareness and Vyne went hand in hand. Every time he was near, it was like my entire being was attuned to him.

Still, I shifted closer, letting my shoulder rest against him.

He lowered himself so that we lay side by side, not quite touching beyond the drape of his wing. His wing formed a canopy, deflecting the punishing wind, and gradually, my shivers calmed. I hovered in that strange half-sleep again, the day's exhaustion pulling me under with awkward, uneven surges of rest.

At some point, I must have drifted into sleep. If I dreamed, I couldn't say of what, only that the shadow of a Drakarn warrior stood over it all.

When dawn finally came, it snuck in on a faint, pewter glow. My eyes blinked open to discover the cloak had been pushed aside in favor of something warmer—Vyne. My cheek tucked against his shoulder; one of his arms curved around my waist, claws splayed over the hem of my shirt. His other arm was beneath my head, his fingers near my ear in a loose, almost protective grip. Even more startling, his tail coiled possessively around my calf.

My pulse thudded in my ears. This was too close, too comforting. His body heat soaked into me, each breath measured and slow. I knew I should recoil, should disengage from the intimacy that threatened to tip over the line if I so much as breathed too hard.

But I didn't. Not right away. I relaxed a fraction, letting the lingering chill recede a bit further. There was no time to waste, but for just one moment, I let myself steal the comfort.

TEN
SELENE

Comfort didn't last long. After a breakfast of more dried rations and the sips of water we could spare, Vyne was on his feet and holding something out to me.

"Here."

I stiffened just slightly at his tone. Cool. Professional. Not at all the sound of a man—alien—who'd wrapped me in his arms overnight like I was precious.

Get a grip, Selene.

He was holding out a blade now, its blackened edges flat against the light that flared over the ridge. The knife gleamed, a sickly edge of reflected heat glinting off its curving, jagged design.

"A souvenir?" I asked, taking refuge in dry humor like an escape route as I took the knife. It was heavier than I expected and rough-textured, carved with distinct grooves that made it feel impossibly deadly.

Vyne cast me a glance, just flat enough to make its point. "A precaution," he said evenly. "These mountains are rife with scavengers. Both of the Drakarn variety, and vicious beasts."

Something flickered uncomfortably in my chest, and I gripped the knife harder. "Got it," I said, a low puff of words meant less as agreement and more as a line drawn under every conversation we weren't about to excavate.

Vyne was scanning the horizon again, his sharp lines settled against the violent sprawl of the ridge behind him. He didn't glance back when his wings gave a flick, catching enough sunlit distortion to create a sudden burst of heavy air between us. He simply turned, every part of him a calculation, threw his next look pointedly at the crevice hugging the edge of nearby crags, and then eased his hand into the curl against one side of his belt.

"I'm going to scout out the area before we leave to make sure we don't encounter any company on our flight. Stay alert," he said. "If something finds you before I'm back ..." He trailed only half a beat too long before finishing, "Scream."

Right. Just what I needed to hear.

"Not sure dramatic death screams are really my style." I angled the blade properly at my side as I stood, though exhaustion made even that feel heavier than it was.

"Scream loud enough, *Zhyvarin*, and you won't die."

He burst into the air before I could ask him what the hell *zhyvarin* meant.

No use lingering on it. I leaned back just enough to close my eyes for a breath or two, the knife resting across my lap like a shield, and tried not to give in to the gnawing sense that, clever blade or not, I didn't belong here.

The suffocating quiet of the plateau stretched around me, leaving me to stew in my own thoughts while the heat bore down on me. I would give almost anything for some shade.

Some small, logical part of my brain told me to conserve energy, to ease my muscles and let the restless ache fade from my joints before I had to move again. But that part of my brain always forgot who it was dealing with—it was the soldier in me that braced, kept the flex of my hands curling and uncurling around Vyne's blade, and sent every nerve into overdrive at the sound of even the faintest crackle of rock sliding somewhere beyond the ridge.

The sound wasn't new. Not really. The mountains were alive in their own way—rocks falling, distant steam geysers erupting with gut-punch force every now and then. But tension didn't leave much room for distinguishing natural from unnatural—not when survival depended on treating every noise as a threat.

And survival was always the game, wasn't it?

I lifted the blade once more, testing its weight in my palm, its smooth handle fitting snugly into the curve of my fingers. There was a grim comfort in the way it fit with every subtle change in my grip—it felt like Vyne knew, somehow, what size and heft I'd need, like this thing had been crafted with some maddeningly intimate knowledge of what fit my hand better than, say, the hand of an average Drakarn.

A sound came again. Louder now.

I sat up straighter, fingers tightening on the hilt as sound rolled over me like a boulder I hadn't been quick enough to dodge. My throat worked past the flat dryness of the air, my pulse climbing its way up to my ears as my senses flared to life.

There was nothing natural about the scrape of claws against stone.

The quickest way to die in unfamiliar territory was to assume you had the upper hand. One misstep, and your throat might end up torn out. I'd seen it before—trainees who wanted to play hero, underestimated an opponent or a situation until it ate them alive.

Literally, in some cases.

The mountain air thickened in my lungs, hemmed in by the heat swirling like smothering mist around the plateau.

There—a flash of movement below the ridge, quick and sharp. My stomach twisted. It wasn't Vyne —too large for him, and it moved wrong. Too slick, too feral.

I dropped into a low stance before my brain fully caught up, bracing one foot instinctively on the uneven rock. Adrenaline hit fast and sharp, slicing through the oppressive heat stretching tight across my ribs.

Assess, position, anticipate.

The first rule of combat. It had been drilled into me in training until it mapped itself into my muscles —not always neat, not always perfect, but ready despite the brutal terrain now pressing in around me.

There was another flicker of motion. Closer this time, clearer in its sharp, bounding trajectory over the blackened rock below.

I swallowed hard and adjusted my grip. My thumb brushed the hilt of the blade, the hilt pressing familiarly against my skin.

The scrape of claws on stone echoed sharply.

The first figure crested the ridge, his hulking frame outlined against the heated shimmer of the air behind it. The light carved shadows over his scaled body, revealing dark, gleaming patches of multicolored scales that reflected the searing sunlight in fractured patterns. His face split wide with a sharp, guttural hiss, exposing rows of curved, serrated fangs that looked built for shredding through anything unfortunate enough to land in their path.

And that tail—thick and scaled like a living whip —lashed with restless precision, the tip twitching as though eager to sink into flesh. It wasn't just a movement of balance but an anticipatory one, alive with violence.

Another followed close behind, snarling low as he scrambled across the uneven ridge, his talons clicking loudly against the stone. His scales were duller than the first, mottled with scars and darkened staining that looked somehow wrong, like old blood that had been absorbed into the flesh. The same unnervingly long tongue flicked out with a sharp twist of his head, tasting the sulfur-heavy air like it could already smell me—like he had singled me out as prey.

More followed behind him.

They were Drakarn.

Too much like Vyne to be mistaken for anything else but filled with so much hate and vicious intent they almost seemed like another species.

They didn't just look like they wanted to kill. They looked like they would enjoy it.

They were circling.

The largest of the group—a massive brute with scales that shimmered like bruised firelight—stepped forward, lowering his head. Heat waves rippled up from the ridge behind him, distorting the violent sprawl of its body to something almost monstrous. Every step brought him closer to me, like he had already decided the next move was mine, but I wouldn't survive to make it. Its wings flared, the membranes semi-translucent against the molten brightness of the landscape.

Some awful instinct within me screamed when his snake-like tongue hissed out again, moving viscously against his fangs before he drew it back into its mouth. A sound escaped it then—a sharp, snarling hiss that vibrated low and guttural through the air before it rose in pitch, slicing like a knife through the oppressive quiet. It was nothing like the commanding tones of Vyne. This was wild, all hunger and rage and malice stripped back to its rawest form.

Think, Selene. Move.

The massive Drakarn lunged without warning, and pure instinct yanked me sideways before his talons could rake across my midsection. I tumbled low, crouching to regain balance as his strike crashed rock where I'd just stood, the impact sending shards of stone skittering across the plateau. My grip on the knife tightened, nerves sparking with electricity.

Before I could adjust fully, another one came barreling toward me from the right—faster, smaller, but no less dangerous. I spun to meet him, feeling every ounce of strain tearing through my ribs as I slashed upward with the knife against his advance. The blade connected cleanly with his lower arm, biting into the gap where softer sinew met rigid plating. The Drakarn staggered briefly, his injured limb snapping backward with a shuddering cry, but the movement didn't slow him for long.

Momentum. Don't lose it.

I dropped to one knee as another lunge—this one viciously fast—sent talons ripping just above my head. My free hand gripped the slick ground as I braced upward and slashed again, the knife biting deep into the sinewy stretch of his leg this time. Dark blood sprayed, hot and metallic smelling, across the rock inches from my face.

The injured Drakarn reeled with a voracious hiss, wings snapping wide and throwing a violent gust of air against me as I rolled away painfully, barely catching myself on the uneven ground.

More were closing in, their distorted shadows flickering across the plateau. A shuddering frustration climbed in my chest alongside pure, searing exhaustion. I hadn't been ready for this. Not for all of them—not for the speed or the raw physicality that turned every motion into a gamble between cautious calculation and blind desperation.

Then the largest one—the brute—moved again.

I stumbled, crashing hard against the craggy rock, though sheer stubborn force kept the knife gripped tight in my hand.

The pack's movements shifted then, slowing but somehow more dangerous.

They had me cornered now. Trapped at the edge of the plateau where the drop below opened like a yawning death sentence.

The brute took another step forward, his claws clicking ominously as he tilted his head. Those slit-pupiled eyes glimmered against the reflected light of the molten rivers below. There was something almost ... amused in its gaze.

If he was going to kill me, he wanted me to feel it first.

Fuck that.

I straightened shakily, muscles burning, but kept

the knife angled upward between us as a defiant snarl tried to pull itself up past my throat. My pulse pounded loud in my ears, stubbornness clawing sharp and vivid through the fear choking my lungs.

If this hellscape wanted a fight, I'd give it one.

The brute surged forward, wings flaring wide. I knew I wasn't fast enough to avoid this one properly —but at the last second, as I sucked in a sharp, desperate breath, a flicker of movement pulled my gaze upward.

And then the air changed.

No—the air cracked.

A massive shadow collided full force with the brute, sending him spiraling sideways into the jagged rock as a shockingly loud snarl burst through the suffocating quiet. It wasn't until the edges of the shadow sharpened—unfolding fast, precise, and rippling wings caked in black heat—that I realized what I was looking at.

Vyne.

He moved so fast it barely registered—the sleek motion of his wings slicing through the stifling air as his tail swung in a sharp arc, knocking one of the smaller Drakarn clean off the plateau.

ELEVEN
VYNE

The scent hit me first.

Hers.

Something darker hung in the air with it; blood, bile, the feral stink of fury unchained. Of Drakarn rage.

My muscles coiled tight, instinct sharpening into something closer to weaponry than thought. Something was wrong.

The ridge came into view faster than I should've managed—faster than the ache clawing at my wings could complain. My descent sliced clean through the air, every violent beat of my wings driving me closer. The landscape blurred, streaks of crimson and volcanic black giving way to brutal clarity as the plateau rushed toward me.

Selene.

If they'd— If she—

No. Don't think. Act.

I saw her as the details burned into place—a momentary impression, devastating for how quickly it tunneled into me. Cornered.

Her back pressed against the ridge's precarious edge, knife raised in a desperate line of defense. Defiance painted every exhausted line of her battered frame, her small human form trembling on the verge of collapse but refusing to yield.

They circled her. Rogues.

Drakarn who'd traded honor for savagery, their movements small, calculated, cruel. Their tongues flicked, claws raking across stone as they prowled closer, vicious intent hanging heavy in the heat.

Not just death. They wanted worse.

The sky all but shattered when I hit them.

The gust from my landing sent two of them sprawling, their bodies slamming against the ridge's unforgiving surface with sickening force. Stone buckled underfoot, splintering as shards cracked outward from where my talons anchored deep.

The third rogue—the largest of the pack—spun toward me, hissing out a sound that was equal parts rage and surprise. His movements were sluggish compared to my strike, his slick, too-bright scales catching nothing but failure as my claws drove deep into the heavily muscled curve of his chest.

The sound he made—a wet, gurgling screech—satisfied something cold inside me.

"You touched her. You die."

My voice grated low, unrestrained. It didn't simply echo across the ridge; it commanded. Final. Absolute. A promise etched into the rock beneath me.

None of them moved fast enough.

The smallest rogue lunged at the edge of my wing—but before he could strike, my tail lashed out, slamming into him with a crash that made him collapse. He dropped first to his knees, then fully forward into the dust, lifeless.

The brute recovered quickly, roaring as he lunged forward with a ferocity born of desperation. Massive claws swiped wide, aiming for my midsection—an attack too clumsy to merit caution. I didn't pull back. Not back. Never.

Pivoting sharply, I darted to the side, the swing of his strike skimming the air I left behind. My wings hammered back fiercely, propelling me straight toward him as I slammed my claws into the side of its maw.

Something crunched. Fangs caught briefly on my gauntleted hand before I tore myself free with a force that sent gore splattering across the rock behind him.

He staggered, stepping back with a mangled snarl, his blood dripping thickly in rough streaks that sizzled against the heat of the ground.

I advanced. My arm shot forward, carving into the column of his throat with exacting force. My weight collided with his bulk, each motion deliberate, powered by bloodlust honed into something sharper than instinct.

The brute swayed, refusing to fall. His massive frame reeked of defiance, but it didn't hold when my tail speared into the connective joint of his wing.

The scream he let out tore through the thick air, primal and broken.

My wings flared wide, anchoring me against his failed resistance as I drove him down. He buckled hard. Collapsing under the crushing combination of clawed strikes and raw, unrelenting weight. As his chest hit the ridge beneath us, he squirmed one last time—half resistance, half instinct pushing him toward survival.

The brute fell silent.

Behind me, the remaining rogue scrambled back, his panic-laced hissing scraping over molten air as he turned to flee.

Two steps.

That's all he got.

My tail hooked sharply into his back leg and dragged it over the splintered ridge. His snarls turned desperate, sharp claws carving scratches into the agonized rock as he fought.

Futile.

"You don't get mercy," I said. My voice was quiet, almost thoughtful, but the edge of it could've cleaved the ridge itself.

My claws sank neatly into his throat. Twist. Tear.

Silence.

I stood over the remains of them, breath dragging through my lungs, the remnants of the fight settling low in my limbs. Scented with blood. With violence.

And underneath it all—her.

Selene.

The heat simmered around me, pulsing sharp and fevered as I straightened. Every inhale dragged currents of heated air into my chest, its weight clinging as though trying to anchor me in the after-math. Her scent threaded through it all, sharper now, intertwined with the adrenaline and ash-slicked air pressing hot onto the ridge.

She was barely standing.

Her back was rigid, though exhaustion nearly buckled her frame. One hand gripped the hilt of the knife I'd given her, her knuckles white where her resolve tried to bleed into the steel. The way she held it—not raised in threat but trembling with raw defiance—was a testament to her. She wasn't fearless; no, she was far too human for that.

But she was breathtaking all the same.

My knife. *My* woman.

The truth of it didn't matter, not now with my blood running hot and battle riding high.

Even bruised with blood streaking the soft edges of her brown skin, she stood like a creature made of fire and spite, still ready—still fighting—even with nothing left to wield but that knife and whatever shards of stubbornness she could cling to.

Her dark eyes darted to me briefly, then away. She wasn't shaking anymore, but her stance betrayed the truth—heels edging into bad footing, muscles braced too tight, her body locked somewhere between ready-collapse and survival instinct.

"You're not hurt."

Not a question. A demand.

Her gaze snapped upward, locking onto mine with a sharpness that would've made a weaker creature falter. Her lips trembled, but only long enough for her to bite down and press them tight against the emotion straining there. Her chest rose unevenly, breath catching before she answered with a force that nearly cracked under the weight of its own stubbornness.

"I'm fine." Her voice was strained. Fractured at the edges.

I didn't believe it for a single burning second.

"You're shaking." The words came out harder than I intended, sharp enough to strike the tension between us, and her response cut back with a biting force that tried masking the cracks beneath it.

"Adrenaline," she said, her chin tipping upward, pride lacing every inch of the stubborn line she drew between us. "That's how it works."

It might've worked—on anyone else. But the brittle flame in her eyes, flickering right alongside every sharp inhale, told me otherwise.

I moved forward again, closing the space with steady steps. She didn't step back. Not fully. But she stiffened, the knife angling between us, more barrier than threat.

I stopped just short of swinging range. Not that I was braced for a fight—no. I'd die before I raised a claw against her, but there was something about the way she planted herself there, stubborn and almost trembling, that made me tread carefully.

Softer. Not weaker, just quieter.

"You don't smell like adrenaline." The observation left my throat rough, my voice barely above a growl, and the way her skin flinched at the sound cut something low through me. "Your fear is soaked into the air. So is the blood."

Her sarcastic laugh cut sharp across the heat, bitter and jagged. "I hadn't noticed."

But her bravado did nothing to mask the tremor trailing through her fingers. The trembling tip of her knife faltered again, though her knuckles stayed white from gripping too tightly.

My gaze swept downward, dragging over her weakening stance, the wobble of her knees where exhaustion rippled through her frame. I searched for blood, for anything hidden in the curve of her arm or the desperate rise of her breath that she might be trying to shield.

Because if she was bleeding unnoticed— If she couldn't even tell ...

"Stop." Her voice cracked against me, breaking harder than the knife she still held like it meant anything. Her free hand rose suddenly, palm lifted toward me like she could push me back with a single word. "Don't look at me like I'm about to fall apart."

Her stubbornness might as well have been a current drawn straight from the molten vein of Volcaryth itself, snapping bright and furious against something more fractured underneath.

I blinked slowly, jaw clenching against the

instinct to bare my teeth in a snarl. My next step was sharp, harder than I meant it to be, but precise enough to close the final stretch of space that separated us.

"Let me see," I said, quieter now but still sharp. The low press of my voice coiled like heat breaking under pressure, and my claws flexed where they hung just within reach of touching her.

"I told you—" she tried, but I silenced her.

"Let me *see*." The growl came unbidden, rough and low, carrying the force of a command she didn't have room to argue with anymore.

I wanted to say it was instinct. Or desperation. But it was neither.

It was something harsher, sharper, thrumming dangerously low in the pulse of my blood.

Her jaw tightened again, her lips pressing together as if she was fighting to anchor herself against more resistance. Her chest rose briefly, enough for her chin to tilt higher, but her defiance cracked under some unspoken, mutual weight that neither of us knew how to place.

She shifted. A step. Small.

Enough.

I moved closer, closing what little distance still lingered. My claws reached carefully—angling for the curve where her shoulder met the sleeve of her shirt even as my senses flared sharper beneath her scent.

Selene stiffened immediately, her muscles tightening, but she didn't pull away. My grip steadied gently—not restraint, not fully, but angled enough to guide her. My gaze swept her shoulders, tracing over the flush of her skin, over the streaked minerals and ash scattered across her arm.

No punctures. No claw marks.

No blood. At least none of hers.

The coil in my chest—tight, suffocating—began to ease around the edges. Even as heat simmered dangerously low beneath each rasping breath.

"You're reckless." My claws uncurled, releasing the tiny sensation of contact they'd kept where her arm burned beneath them. I didn't move far. Didn't withdraw.

My hand remained there a moment longer than it should've, hovering just near the edge of where her steady defiance began softening into frayed exhaustion. "Reckless," I muttered again, quieter this time. Something between relief and accusation wedged itself thick into my throat as every nerve threatened to fray. "*And stubborn.* I told you to yell for help."

Her strength—astonishing in its raw, stubborn humanity during the ambush—was fading. Here, under the suffocating quiet that followed the fight and the crushing heat of Volcaryth's ridge, she was cracking.

My claws ached with the need to steady her.

"I—" she began, her voice uneven and splintered, barely piecing itself together. Her weight shifted, grounding slightly against the ridge beneath her feet —but just barely. "I didn't have time to think. Those things ..." Her words faltered, lost somewhere in the raw scrape of memory and the overwhelming chaos still clawing at her veins. "I didn't—"

"Stop."

My voice came sharper than I intended, biting through the fragile space she'd carved for her protest. The flicker of softness lurking in her defiance startled into something wide-eyed.

"If you think I need an excuse, save it," I growled, every syllable taut with restrained weight. "You're alive. You fought back. That's the only thing keeping this entire ridge from being painted with scavenger blood."

Her lips twitched—the hint of a frown brushing against her brow before she leaned into a sharp, uneven laugh. Bitter, almost broken. "Then what's all that?" she nodded to the splatter left by one of the beasts before I cast him off the plateau.

The quip fell flat, though, trailing off somewhere beneath the heat stretching between our bodies like a fault line ready to rip wide open. Her gaze twitched downward briefly—not submission; no, not her—but something tangled and cautious. Maybe even strained. Her grip on the knife slackened before dropping entirely.

The blade clattered against the stone.

"You're trembling," I said again. Not accusing her this time, just noticing, just reading her the same way I read every shift in battle, except this war was entirely different. Entirely maddening. "And it's not nothing."

"I didn't come out of that unscathed," she replied, cryptic but unconvincing. The false strength wavering over the brittle layers of her voice only sharpened my awareness further. "I'll be fine. I just need—"

Her hand rose briefly, brushing across her face as though she could physically press the lingering panic aside. "I need—" She stopped again. Her line of thought broke with a sharp breath before looking back up at me.

Her expression was fiercer than I'd anticipated. Fiercer, too, than I was prepared for.

"I'll deal with it," she said, quieter now, but with every ounce of strength her emotions had left to offer. "My fear. My shaking. All of it. It's mine."

"No."

The word came without thought—without restraint. Low but deliberate, sharper than the hiss of hot air pouring from the distant geysers below us. Every sharp instinct, every fraying edge of my mind burned in protest against her words, against the thin walls she attempted to build between us.

Her gaze snapped sharply upward, dark and unyielding as disbelief flickered there. "What?"

"Give it to me," I murmured, claws twitching where they hovered near my sides. "Your pain, your exhaustion—it's what I'm here for."

TWELVE
VYNE

I stopped myself.

The edge of my tongue scraped against my fangs, heat surging up my throat as something inside me howled at the thin, slipping leash I'd kept anchored around the truth.

Her expression hardened again—a flare of defiance. "I'm not something to be—"

"Gods." My hand shot forward—not sharply, not in anger, but steeped in the raw frustration she pushed into every space between us. My claws brushed against her shoulder, feather-light, then froze when I felt her flinch beneath the soft but unyielding pressure.

Every ounce of me recoiled, a surge of self-control wrenching through my chest. But before I could pull back fully, her own movement stopped me. She leaned, imperceptibly but undeniably, just barely toward me. When my grip stilled—steady but quiet along the curve of her arm—she didn't step away.

I couldn't stop looking at her. At the fragile tremor carved into her jawline, at the roughness blooming over her cracked lips, at her lashes dusted with the ever-present ash streaking the rest of her face.

Her scent—fates above, her scent—threw every part of me into restless chaos. I burned brighter than the veins twisting deep through Volcaryth's blackened heart.

Krysfruit. Smoked salt. Her. Always her.

"Selene," I murmured, without meaning to. Her name cracked through my throat, more growl than word. "You don't get to carry it alone."

She stiffened a little beneath my touch, her gaze flickering over my expression like she was trying to read something there. "I do. I have to. I—"

"You don't," I ground out, cutting her protest short. My head dipped lower, the motion instinctual, undeniable. The words I needed wouldn't come— couldn't. Nothing could bridge the aching space threatening to splinter everything. "Not from me."

Her lips parted as if to argue or push me back into whatever tactical distance she thought she needed for logic to breathe between us. But nothing came.

And the sound of that silence was shattering. Deafening. Ripping whatever restraint I had left into useless fragments.

Her scent sharpened against me in unbearable waves.

I lowered my head without thinking. Closer. Dangerous. Every part of me screamed at once—not just desire, not just instinct, but something brighter, terrible in its force.

Her knees dipped, shifting her weight forward, closer to mine. And her breath—ragged and too quick —hitched just enough to shatter the careful tension strangling the ridge.

"Selene," I growled again, hoarse and rough, a surrender wrapped in her name.

Control was gone. Fully. Terrifyingly.

I kissed her.

It wasn't careful. It wasn't soft. The moment was too raw for any of that. My lips crushed against hers before I could think myself around it; before I had time to stop and consider what it might cost.

Her warmth bled into me; her taste hit the back of my fangs—salt and heat and something maddeningly sweet beneath it all—and everything unraveled.

She gasped against me, surprise giving way to

something low and startled, but she didn't pull back. She moved toward me instead. Her lips, soft but cracked, parted beneath mine, not yielding, but answering.

Her hands—uncertain and shaking from adrenaline—caught the edge of my armor, trembling before curling tighter. The heat of them—small, human, too fragile—seared through even the thick, fire-forged metal, cutting into me sharper than any clawed strike ever had.

My claws flexed briefly. Just enough to linger near her sleeve and then tighten ever so slightly, careful but protective, just shy of helpless.

Her taste.

It built heat behind my ribs and poured tension into every inch of me I couldn't anchor. My tongue flicked against her bottom lip—primal, entirely unbidden, entirely maddening in its sensitivity—and that was it. The last thread of restraint frayed itself to ash.

I angled my head, deepening the kiss until her breath hitched sharply against mine, a trembling gasp escaping her throat as her hands tightened against my scales. Not resistance. Not anymore. Her grip wasn't something born of fear or hesitation; it was something closer to instinct, to need, raw and unfiltered in its desperate hold on me.

Her lips moved tentatively beneath mine, uncertain at first, but growing bolder. Her body tipped infinitesimally closer, shoulders rising with every fractured breath racing between us. The brush of her fingers clinging to the scaled edges of my neck made something deep in my chest curl tight, heat sparking low and dangerous where her nails raked against flesh.

Gods below, she wasn't pulling away.

Sensations poured into me in waves. The tremor in her frame as it eased closer. The scent of her, impossibly rich and sharper now with her sweat. The sound she made, a soft, involuntary noise escaping her throat, when my claws shifted, just barely, to ghost along the curve of her neck.

My restraint wasn't just fraying—it was disintegrating.

What was left of the logical side of me screamed to pull back, to stop giving in to the raw instinct and rein in control before everything tipped past the point of no return. But the connection between us was already burning too bright, too consuming. Her scent invaded every inch of my senses. Her taste lingered on every edge of my tongue, more potent than any flame Volcaryth had ever birthed into existence.

I couldn't think.

Only feel.

My claws, still trembling from restraint, flexed where they cupped the slope of her shoulder. It wasn't enough. Couldn't be. The undercurrent pouring heat straight into my blood demanded more.

I slid one hand lower until my claws hovered delicately at the edge of her waist, the thin fabric of her shirt a useless barrier against the blistering heat growing between us. Her breath stuttered as soon as she felt the shift, her chest rising sharply against mine before melting into the pull of my weight anchoring her closer.

Her lips parted farther, and the brush of her tongue sent electricity sparking up my spine, setting fire to every thread of self-control I still had.

I growled—low, deep, possessive—a sound I barely recognized as mine.

Her response? She trembled, yes, but not from fear. Instead, her body leaned forward, tipping against me as though drawn into the same unbearable pull threatening to unmake me. Her nails dug against the curve where my neck met my shoulder, testing the edge of my scales, and the subtle scratch of it sent another shudder rippling through me.

Something feral clawed its way to the surface. Buried for too long, ignored for longer. The sheer rightness of her against me—of her taste, her touch, her breath threading into mine—forced every sharp edge of my instincts into blinding want.

She fit against me too perfectly.

I broke the kiss, though it felt more like wrenching myself out past the event horizon of something unstoppable. My lips dragged away slowly, reluctantly, while every inch of my body fought the loss. I stopped when only the smallest space separated us, our shared breaths still mixing in shallow, uneven rhythm.

My wings trembled, the strain of holding them tight against my back just as agonizing as the distance I now forced between us. Her scent—gods, her scent swarmed my airways, still heavy, still drowning me in her.

Her lips—kiss-swollen and perfect—parted as though she wanted to say something. But the words didn't come. Only her breath emerged, soft and battered, her chest rising too fast and too unevenly as her heartbeat thumped loudly enough for my height-ened senses to catch all of it.

Her eyes burned into mine, wide and searching, her expression wide with an emotion I was too afraid to name. Confusion. Need. Awe. Fear. All of it swirled beneath the ash-dusted surface of her gaze.

"*Zhyvarin*," I rasped.

It wasn't just a word. It was the name I'd

dreamed up for her in the nights when I couldn't ignore what she truly was to me, when the dreams wouldn't let me go. It was lightning, scoring its way through my chest—a sound shaped by fate, dragged from the deepest corner of whatever I was becoming beneath her touch.

She blinked. Once. Twice. Then something sharp sparked in her expression again—less confusion now, but caution. Her brow furrowed as realization caught up to the shock threatening to carve its way through every sharp edge between us. Slowly, her hands loosened from their grip on my scales, her fingers trembling as they hovered, uncertain, in the burning air between us.

"What—" Her voice broke, soft at first, then sharper, biting out against the searing quiet surrounding us.

A thousand answers burned on the tip of my tongue.

None dared leave my mouth.

Instead, I reached for her wrist, careful to catch it lightly, my claws brushing just barely over the fragile edge of her pulse. One step closer. Just one. Just enough for my gaze to find hers again, unflinching.

"*Zhyvarin.*"

The word slipped out again, unbidden but undeniable, soft and soaked in reverence.

Her brow furrowed again, the bite of defiance curling over her lips. "What?"

I couldn't explain. Couldn't risk it. Not now. Not with every nerve in me still locked between the ache to hold her and the fear of breaking something irreparable.

"Never mind," I muttered, though the weight in my voice betrayed the words as a lie.

It did matter. More than anything. And the way her gaze lingered then flickered back to my lips, her own still trembling, told me she knew it, even if she couldn't say it.

The silence between us coiled tighter, broken only by the distant hiss of geysers erupting against the ridge. My claws loosened reluctantly against her wrist, slipping back into the void that lingered between warmth and absence.

She didn't move right away. She stayed there, shoulders caught between tension and uncertainty, her frame too frayed to dare finishing whatever storm of thought hung in her expression.

THIRTEEN
SELENE

Vyne walked beside me, his gait steady and sure, like the uneven rock beneath us posed no challenge at all. There wasn't so much as a hitch in his pace.

I tried not to let my gaze linger on his tightly folded wings or glinting scales. Not when there were enough reasons already to keep my attention fixed squarely on the crumbling path ahead. The terrain wasn't the only thing I had to watch for.

Two days.

That was how long it'd been since the kiss.

Two days since he'd breached every armored wall I'd thought I'd built, and I'd been stupid enough to kiss him back like breaking apart beneath him was inevitable.

Now, there was nothing between us except the

grind of rock underfoot, the heavy press of the air, and the occasional sound of tremors rumbling under the surface.

Maybe I should have been grateful for the silence. But it only made the memory harder to ignore.

I yanked my focus forward, sparing no more than a second to tighten the scarf clinging against my face to help block out the rancid air. Each step dragged a little harder than the last, exhaustion pressing in sharper than the heat clinging to the air. Vyne didn't even look winded. His focus stayed locked onto the path ahead, scanning every jagged cut in the mountainous landscape.

I cleared my throat. "Do we even know where this stuff grows?"

"Unstable ground," he replied, his voice as even and unshaken as his movements. "Anywhere the earth has split wide or the heat vents through cracks. Vyrathis will stand out from the surrounding rock."

That was frustratingly non-specific. Just vague terrain descriptions paired with every possible hazard the Harrovan Mountains had to offer.

Perfect.

"Helpful," I said, dry as the air threatening to crack my lips. My sarcasm felt like the only weapon I had left.

It earned nothing more than the faintest glance from him, his brow lifting in unbothered acknowledgment. "Would you like me to conjure the plant from thin air instead?"

"If you could do that, you should have tried three days ago," I shot back.

The corner of his mouth twitched—so faint that it might've been melted into the ambient heat of this place, except I recognized it for what it was. Not quite a smile, not quite not. And damn it, I hated how it sent some small sizzle through me.

This awareness of Vyne was going to be the death of me.

Dragging my attention back to the ridge ahead, I kept my pace steady. The ground was shifting more there, the blackened rock glittering with oppressive heat. Treacherous footing at best. But that's when I saw it—a shimmer caught in the light, something alive amid this endless stretch of dead stone.

"Wait," I said, sharper than I meant to. My hand twitched vaguely toward the glint of color as I slowed. "Is that ...?"

There was no hesitation in how Vyne moved. Before I could say anything else, he stepped ahead of me, his wings shifting as he assessed the terrain. His claws flexed against the rock, finding safe purchase where I'd struggle.

I followed him anyway. Sitting still had never been my thing, and I wasn't going to let him handle this alone.

There it was—low and barely there against a black fissure: vyrathis.

Its thin leaves shone with a metallic sheen, curling outward like it had grown in defiance of the oppressive heat swallowing the landscape. The glow of the plant was a small pocket of alien color against the harsh black of the mountainside.

"Shit, that's it," I breathed, tension easing just long enough for relief to rush in sharply.

"Careful." Vyne's voice came low, guarded. He crouched near the plant, his claws hovering just above the ground. "There's a gas pocket nearby," he said, his voice quieter now, his wings pressing outward in readiness. "The ground's unstable underneath."

"Great," I muttered, irritation vibrating louder than fear in my voice. "The one thing we actually need, and the whole mountain's ready to swallow us for it."

I crouched down beside him, the vyrathis close enough that I could feel the heat emanating from its fragile leaves. My hand moved toward my pack, fingers brushing against the stiff edge of the container Rachel had given me before we left.

I crouched at the plant's edge, my fingers gripping the container with care, keeping it angled just right. My free hand moved toward a small tool strapped to my thigh—a sturdy but lightweight blade meant for shearing samples cleanly. I worked quickly, each motion precise as I trimmed the silvery leaves away from the delicate stems.

The air was thinner there, sharper somehow, though I couldn't tell if it was my mind playing tricks on me or the gas Vyne had warned about seeping up from somewhere deeper in the mountain below. My pulse jumped, but I forced it down. Focus. I didn't need to think about imaginary disasters when the real ones were waiting just underfoot.

"Selene."

His voice cut through the thin air. A warning. I froze, my hand hovering mid-motion with the blade angled near one of the stems.

"What?" I asked.

He didn't respond immediately. Instead, his eyes locked onto the fissure directly beside where I crouched. His wings twitched as the sound of shifting rock rumbled low beneath us.

"Don't move," he snapped, firm enough that it left no room for argument.

I froze.

My grip tightened on the container in my hand,

and my pulse hammered against the silence stretching between us. Vyne's claws flexed as he stepped closer. The scrape of rock shifted under his weight, audible even over the heat-warped air squeezing the mountainside.

Vyne was all precision, anchoring into the nearer edge of stone while his tail wrapped around a thicker outcrop behind us for extra support. It was painfully clear just how much stronger his body was than mine —as if the terrain itself bent beneath his touch, unwilling to argue against the force he carried in every movement.

He applied pressure to the fissure nearest the plant, testing it. His wings shifted again, catching currents of air rising from somewhere deeper in the rock. I didn't realize I'd been holding my breath until he finally straightened and nodded at me.

"Go on," he said, the protective angle of his wings shielding me from whatever unseen threat still lurked.

I resumed my work, my focus tightening as I clipped the last of the vyrathis stems and sealed them carefully in the container. The silvery surface of the leaves glinted, catching patterns of light that seemed almost too delicate for a place like this.

"We need more," I said, rising carefully from my crouch.

Vyne's green eyes flicked toward the container in my hands, and for a moment, there was something like relief written in the sharp lines of his expression. Not warmth, not exactly—but close enough to knock me off-center.

My eyes darted down to his lips, and I squeezed them shut before any thoughts about what those lips could do rose up.

Too late.

Shoving the container back into the secured pocket of my pack, I straightened, wincing at the ache settling into my shoulders.

Without a word, Vyne moved closer, his claws brushing against the ledge for balance as his hand extended toward me. His large frame cast long shadows over the tiny ridge, and his gaze fixed on me with that same irritating intensity he always carried.

I hesitated, just for a moment. Then, gripping his offered hand, I caught his wrist with mine and allowed him to guide me away from the edge.

The vyrathis was easier to spot the second time. And the third. I lost track of time, but the ache in my legs and the burn in my lungs told me it had been hours. My bag was full to bursting with vyrathis, container stuffed full.

It had to be enough.

The healers would live. If we got it home to them in time.

Vyne put down a marker at the biggest bed of the plant, a stake in the ground with a brightly covered piece of cloth tied to the end that could be spotted from the air so Drakarn from Scalvaris would know where to look if we had to send them back for even more.

We'd done it.

For now, at least, it had to be enough.

The ground was growing more unstable by the minute, and we couldn't linger. I stepped into Vyne's arms and let him launch me into the air as we began our flight home.

The place we stopped at wasn't much of a campsite, but it was flat, and that was good enough for me. It was carved out of a small space in the mountainside, shielded by a curve of sharp black rock that jutted outward like broken teeth.

Heat shimmered across every surface, but now the air softened just a little compared to the suffocating press from earlier. I wouldn't call it breathable, but I wasn't choking on every inhale now either.

Small mercies.

Our packs were slumped against the outcrop, their rough fabric streaked with ash and dirt from the endless journey. I collapsed against the rock wall, letting out a long, unsteady breath as I tugged the scarf from my face now that the rock was blocking some of the worst gusts of sulfurous winds. The deceptively light vyrathis container rested in my lap.

The trip wasn't over—not even close—but for the first time since setting out, the sense of triumph outweighed the exhaustion clinging to every single muscle I had.

Vyne moved a few feet away, crouching and holding onto the stone like it was nothing. He didn't look worn out—hell, he didn't even look inconvenienced. His movements lacked any sluggishness as he pulled a water flask free, uncapping it with the same ease he carried in every action.

"Could you at least pretend you're as exhausted as I am?" I muttered, craning my neck to glance over at him. The consequences of the flight and search pressed against my ribs, but irritation felt like a better distraction than lingering on how much energy I'd burned.

Vyne paused, mid-motion, then glanced at me with a lift of his brow. "Would it help?"

"Yeah," I shot back, quick enough to feel the pull of amusement creep into my voice. "Solidarity and all that."

He tilted his head, expression calm but a bit edged. For just a moment, I thought I caught the bare flicker of something like humor somewhere beneath all the unreadable layers he wore like a shield.

"Noted."

I huffed out a shallow breath, leaning my head back and letting my gaze wander past him to the horizon beyond our fragile little camp. The Harrovan peaks stretched endlessly, their silhouettes rising against waves of twisting heat and sulfuric haze. Everything about this place was wrong—hostile.

Beautiful, sure, but ready to remind you just how easily it could kill you.

I slid the vyrathis container into one of the pouches in my pack, protecting it from the harsh environment. I made myself linger on the process—adjusting, tying the straps—anything to keep my hands busy. But when I stood, shaking the tension out of my legs, I swore my movements pulled his attention again, heavy, steady, and impossible to ignore.

"You should rest."

His voice broke through my thoughts more firmly this time, less suggestion and more instruction. When I glanced back toward him, he'd finally shifted out of that perfect crouch, standing in a smooth motion that sent his wings flexing. His stance was too steady, his gaze too focused, and I hated that the sharp edge of it made my pulse falter.

"What does it look like I'm doing?" I snapped.

His narrowed gaze didn't budge. The huff that followed was subtle, barely audible, but it cut all the same. Without saying anything, Vyne stepped closer —his tall frame shadowing me.

"Selene." The sound of my name wasn't harsh. He said it with just enough force to dig under every fragile excuse I wanted to give. "You've done enough."

I swallowed hard, the air clinging between us too heavy. This close, Vyne wasn't just sharp edges and brutal efficiency anymore—there was something else to him. Something softer, buried beneath the skin of his alien presence like a broken ember glow, threatening to burn brighter the longer I looked.

The moment pressed down like everything else in this place—the heat, the sulfur, the rocks underfoot. But this—this was heavier in a way you couldn't run from. I felt the sharp edges of it cutting through every breath, twisting tightly as Vyne's gaze stayed locked on me.

"You've done too much," he repeated. His voice dipped lower this time, rough but steady, like he could force the air itself to yield. "Rest. Now."

Something flared in me—not defiance, exactly.

Not quite. Just the reflexive need to push back against whatever told me I couldn't keep going.

Pride was a hell of a thing. I wasn't about to let it go.

"I told you, I'm fine." The words came out sharp, but not sharp enough to cut through the tension clinging stubbornly between us. "We rest here for a few hours and then head out."

Vyne didn't step back. Of course he didn't. I hated how steady he was; hated the way that same steadiness made something underneath my walls crack.

He tilted his head, his expression shadowed but calm, like he was holding back more than I could ever read. The sharp line of his jaw twitched, dragging every inch of my focus straight to him.

"You're lying," he said simply. Blunt. No malice. Just a cutting sort of truth that landed harder because of how quietly he wielded it.

Something snapped. Exhaustion, maybe, or frustration from how tightly he'd held me under that unreadable gaze. Either way, I exhaled sharply, letting the angry, restless part of me rise to the surface.

"Yeah? Well, we can't all be untouchable super-warriors." My voice cracked just slightly at the edges, but I twisted the words into a dry sneer, hoping they'd be sharp enough to hold their own weight. "Let a girl have some damned pride."

"I'm not untouchable," he said, his voice quieter this time. But something in the way he said it—sharp-edged in a way it didn't need to be—made the hair along the back of my neck lift.

His claws shifted at his sides, the restraint in the motion all the more noticeable because it was too controlled. Like something far deeper simmered just beneath his composed surface. Something real.

He took another step forward, closing the already narrow space between us, and my first instinct was to stiffen. Not out of fear, but because the weight of his presence—sharp and focused, frayed but unyielding—felt like it might crush me if I let it.

"You're not weak," he said firmly, the words catching me off guard enough to throw me silent. His green eyes pinned me in place, their intensity like a wrecking ball through every wall I'd carefully built. "But even the strongest need their rest. We wait out the night. Push now and we might break."

My throat worked against the dryness pressing in, the heat running rough fingers against every inhale. His words clung tighter than the sulfur to the back of my mouth, and for half a second, I didn't have the energy to fight them off.

"That some lesson they teach you in Drakarn warrior school?" My tone slipped somewhere between sarcasm and bitterness. But the edge of my voice cracked, betraying me when I least wanted it to.

"No," he said without hesitation. His gaze stayed soft—not in its strength, but in the way it didn't waver, didn't narrow the way it might if his patience was thin. "It's something I learned because I didn't. Not soon enough."

That admission hit differently—quieter, smaller, but sharp all the same. He didn't elaborate, and I couldn't bring myself to ask. The space between us hung too heavy for words to do anything but pull everything tighter.

I shifted on my feet, trying not to let the air clawing its way between my ribs sound too uneven.

But Vyne didn't let me drag myself away too far. He moved again—not a full step this time, just enough that the edge of his hand brushed against my arm.

Not forceful. Not demanding. Just *there*. Subtle.

And stupidly, infuriatingly steady.

I didn't pull away. I wanted to. Wanted to shove the strange weight of his presence out of my space until I could think clearly again. But the pull it created kept me frozen where I stood.

That same steadiness in him left me undone.

Before I could second-guess the sharp, restless twist building in me, I moved.

The decision hit like an earthquake. Sudden. Destructive. My arms lifted, looping around his neck without ceremony, hugging him close. My pulse hammered against the hollow space carved between us—far from calm but no longer lost to hesitation.

Vyne froze.

For a fraction of a second, it felt like I'd crossed some unspoken fault line between us, and my stomach twisted with uncertainty. But then his hand shifted—his claws ghosting lightly against my side before they curved, careful and caring, to rest just against the small of my back. Not pushing. Not needing to.

Just keeping me steady.

His body, all too solid, didn't lean all the way into me, but his wings curved inward, their outline enough to block out the fading glow of the barren landscape around us. The motion felt unintentional —like he hadn't even noticed himself doing it—but it was enough to set something fragile alight inside me.

His heat should've burned hotter than the magma tearing through Volcaryth beneath us. But it didn't. It didn't hurt at all.

It felt like relief. Like safety.

When I finally let my head tilt upward, the sharp edge of his carved features came into focus—closer than they'd ever been. His breath brushed against my skin, scattering along the small spaces too narrow for heat to settle in fully.

And then he kissed me.

FOURTEEN
SELENE

His mouth tasted like promises and burnt honey.

Not the saccharine stuff people baked into pastries; this was darker. Charcoal bitter and still a bit sweet. I gasped into the kiss, fingers clawing the scales of his neck, their edges biting into my palms. His claws shredded the rock wall behind me, shards raining down around us. Heat radiated from his chest in waves, almost too much to bear.

His heat was a shield, pushing back the icy dread I carried for the healers back in Scalvaris. Just for a moment, I could forget the sickness, the uncertainty, and embrace what it felt like to feel safe.

To feel *alive*.

I didn't know which was louder—the geysers vomiting steam below or the jackhammer of my pulse. My spine ground against the stone as his wings snapped open, blotting out the hellscape's fading glare.

His tongue—long, relentless, perfect—flicked against the seam of my lips. I opened on a broken noise, letting him devour me like I'd been starved for this exact flavor of ruin. The growl vibrating against my mouth wasn't human. Wasn't gentle. His hips pinned me hard.

I wanted more.

Fear coiled low in my belly, a sharp reminder that I was playing with fire—a fire I wasn't sure I could control. But it was a beautiful fire, and my better judgement could take a backseat for once.

The rumble in his chest deepened. One clawed hand let go of the wall to grip my hip, talons careful but the pressure bruising. His tail lashed, gouging fresh ruts into the mountainside.

His pupils were narrow slits, dark shards splitting golden irises. Nostrils flared, drinking my scent like I was the first clean air he'd tasted in forever. My hands shook where they clung to him, torn between shoving him back and dragging him closer until our bodies fused.

"Vyne," I rasped, voice stripped raw.

His thumb brushed my jaw, calloused pad rasping over split skin. "You're shaking."

"Adrenaline crash." I bared my teeth in something too wild to be a smile. "Human thing. We don't usually tongue-fuck walking furnaces when we're hanging off mountains."

A muscle twitched along his jaw. His gaze dropped to my mouth, and I realized my lip had split. I didn't know if it was from the harsh air or his fangs. His growl returned, lower now, as he closed the distance. I braced.

He licked the wound.

The flat of his tongue dragged from my chin up to almost my nose. My breath hitched, nails carving trenches between his shoulder scales. He groaned, the vibration rattling my ribs, and did it again.

"Salt," he murmured against flesh. "Sweet."

It wasn't just lust now. It was possession, a claim. A shiver wracked me, not entirely unpleasant.

"Infection risk," I choked, clinging to medic-mode like a lifeline. "Your mouth's dirtier than a field medic's—fuck!"

Blunt fangs grazed my earlobe. The hand on my hip slid around to grip my ass, hauling me flush against him. Every scaled inch scorched. The thick ridge of his cock pressed through our clothes, that unnatural fleshy tip writhing against me.

"Still scared, *Zhyvarin*?"

The alien word rolled against my neck. I didn't know it. Didn't care. The ledge tilted or maybe my brain short-circuited as his tail coiled around my calf, tip stroking a path above my ankle.

"Terrified," I lied, raking nails down the groove of his spine. "Can't wait to see how you devour me."

God, I *was* terrified.

I was barreling headlong toward a disaster I wasn't sure I could avoid. But I couldn't show it. Couldn't give him that power. So I told him the truth in the voice of a lie, pushing him to the edge, hoping he'd pull me back. Or maybe that he'd push me over.

He laughed and reclaimed my mouth, and it felt like breathing after being held underwater. For once, I didn't care about anything other than him and me; that was what terrified me. The kiss was surrender and conquest, all teeth and dominance. I bit down hard and felt the metal of the barbell in his tongue.

He snarled, wings battering the cliff face as he spun us, pinning me against the heated stone his body had shielded.

Ash clung to the sweat-slick planes of his chest, collecting around shining nipple rings. My shirt hung in ribbons.

"Mine." The declaration seared my throat.

The mountain quaked beneath us. I didn't answer.

Didn't need to.

His claws froze holding the shredded remains of

my bra, the curved tip trembling millimeters from the clasp. The tremor in his hand would've been invisible if my chest weren't flush against his, feeling the live-wire tension corded through his muscles. My smile felt like a blade—sharp, defensive, honed on decades of triage bravado.

"Need help?"

I dragged my nails down the ridged valleys between his back scales, savoring the full-body shudder it ripped from him. His green scales glistened under Volcaryth's fevered glow.

Vyne's growl quaked through my sternum. "Cease testing me."

"Funny," I breathed, rolling my hips to grind against the throbbing ridge of his cock still trapped under his pants. "I thought warriors lived for challenges."

His gaze dropped to my exposed chest, pupils swallowing the last slivers of yellow. Sweat pooled in the hollow of his throat. My tongue darted out, traitorous, and his restraint shattered.

Blunt fangs scraped my collarbone—not a bite, a brand. Claws cinched my hips, lifting me until my legs locked around his waist. Sharp stone gnawed my shoulders, the bite dull compared to the furnace of his scaled torso.

"Don't," he rasped against my sternum, tongue

lapping salt from my cleavage. The tip seared a path down my breast.

My laugh broke into a gasp as I felt his tail climb up my thigh. The ridged underside ground against my inner knee while the tip pricked a warning trail up my calf.

I fisted the dark hair at his nape, wrenching his head back. "Then quit treating me like I'll shatter."

Feral light ignited his gaze. A claw split the band on my chest, shredding the bra's last threads. The material fluttered downward. His palms—scaled, searing—claimed my breasts, testing their give against his callouses.

"Yes," he grated, reverence roughened by lust. A claw-tip circled my nipple, catching just enough to sting. I arched into the burn, and he groaned, canines gleaming. "Say it."

I nipped at his neck, trying for anything I could reach. His hips pressed me harder against the cliff wall, tail teasing my legs wider. "Make me."

His claws took care of my pants, exposing every part of me. Bitter air kissed my thighs as he shredded fabric.

Breath scorched my ear. "*Zhyvarin.*"

That word. It sent a spike of heat through me.

His tail was a fucking menace. And I loved it.

The ridged underside ground slow circles over my sex, each stroke making me shudder.

"More," I begged.

Vyne's snarl vibrated through me as he fell to his knees, and his tongue—fuck, that endless, wanton tongue and the metal nub within it—speared against me. He inhaled sharply, wings flaring, nose buried in the slick heat between my legs.

"Hot," he growled, the word mangled by fangs. Claws pricked my waist, blunt tips threatening bruises. "You burn."

I couldn't think beyond the feelings. His tongue flattened against me in one all-consuming swipe.

Lightning.

My spine arched, a shattered scream tearing free. He growled—possessive, feral—and continued the motion. Again. Again. The wet slap of muscle on flesh echoed off stone, rhythm syncopated by my ragged gasps.

"Fuck—Vyne—!"

He jerked, a sound like splitting stone erupting from his chest. The tail and tongue at my core stroked harder, ridges snagging swollen flesh. I came apart with a choked wail, thighs squeezing against him as reality splintered into shards.

He didn't relent.

The coil snapped again before I could breathe,

his tongue now devoting obscene focus to my nerves. My nails found the membranous gap between his wing joints, gripping delicate tissue.

"Again." The command left his throat raw.

I broke—body bowed, vision going white. The orgasm ripped through me, wringing a sob from my chest. Vyne finally withdrew, chin glistening, eyes void-black pits.

The fleshy hood of his cock twitched, weeping indecent pre-cum.

Where had his pants gone? I didn't care.

I stared at the scaled monster, vein-like ridges pulsing under strained flesh. Before fear could take root, I took hold of the base.

This was new. Something both alien and ... intimate. Not just his touch, but seeing him so completely unleashed, so vulnerable. With the fear came a heady rush of power and ownership.

He froze.

The strange tip curled toward my grip, the alien appendage brushing my knuckles. Velvet-soft. Alive. Madness overrode survival instinct. He'd tasted me. Turnabout was only fair.

Vyne recoiled. "No." The denial strangled itself. He tried pulling back, but I tightened my hold, thumb smearing slick across the slit. His tail spasmed around my thigh. "Can't be ... gentle," he rasped, jaw clenched hard enough to fracture. "Need you."

"Then fucking take me."

He hissed, claws raking across rock above my skull. Then he grabbed only my hips and hooked one of my legs around him.

The first thrust shattered me.

He buried himself to the hilt, the alien girth of him stretching in ways no human anatomy allowed. I gasped out his name, nails tracing the scales between his wings. His cock pulsed—a living thing, veined shaft throbbing in me.

"Fuck—!"

He didn't withdraw. Didn't move. Just hovered, trembling, tail coiled around my thigh like a steel cable.

"*Zhyvarin.*" That word, that special name for me, sounded like a prayer in his throat. Damnation. Worship.

I answered by driving my heel into the back of his knee. "Please."

He growled and dragged out slowly. Agonizing. The scaled base of his shaft stroked against my sex, each ridge striking sparks. His cock's swollen lip peeled away with a lewd pop, leaving the sensitized flesh throbbing.

"Need ... you ..." His claws cratered the ledge above my head.

"Try." I locked my ankles at the small of his back, yanking him home.

He sheathed himself with a snarl, the snap of his hips rocking my spine against basalt. The fleshy hood fluttered against me, alive, as if it had its own rabid pulse. Pleasure scorched up my nerves, white-hot and vicious. I bit his shoulder, flesh and scales flooding my mouth, and he groaned, the vibration shredding my last tether to sanity.

"Look." He wrenched my chin down.

His scaled hips pistoned. The tip of his cock arched upward with each withdrawal, glistening head questing for my clit like a starved beast. Alive. Ravenous. His claws nearly drew blood at my hips, the sting dissolving under the ache pooling in my gut.

"Vyne—I can't—"

"Can." Fangs scraped my jaw. "Take it. Take me."

The ledge quaked beneath us.

"Shit—!"

His wings thundered open, hauling us backward as stone crumbled. We slammed into the opposing wall, his forearm cushioning my skull. The impact drove him even deeper.

A supernova burst behind my eyelids. My spine arched off the rock as the orgasm tore through me, convulsive and raw. He roared, hips stuttering, release scalding my insides.

"*Zhyvarin.*" His forehead pressed to mine, the word a fractured oath. "Mine."

His tail coiled tighter, underside grinding that spot as he wrung my orgasm dry. I thrashed, oversensitive and broken apart, but his claws pricked my hips, forcing me to take every drop.

When reality staggered back, we were a knot of limbs and heaving breath. Vyne's forehead pressed to mine, his purr vibrating through my marrow. His tail flicked against me, flexing lazily.

"Mine," he rasped again, quieter. Surrender. Demand.

I laughed, the sound stripped to bone. My tongue was tied in too many knots to say anything in response.

FIFTEEN
VYNE

Selene lay tangled against me, her breathing uneven but slowing into something calm. Sweat slicked her skin, the salty tang of it lingering where her pulse beat faintly at her neck. Her warmth pressed into mine, every soft edge of her fitting against the sharp, unyielding lines of me. My hand rested low on her hip, claws carefully curved back because I didn't trust them—not with her like this. Fragile. Human.

Mine.

The thought struck, sharp as any blade. It rooted itself too deeply, twisting through me with brutal certainty.

Mine.

And fates take me, nothing had ever burned quite like the satisfaction wrapped up in that word.

Her dark hair clung in damp, chaotic waves to her skin, streaked with ash and grit stolen from this unforgiving landscape. And still, nothing—not Volcaryth's heat, not the volcanic terrain threatening to destroy us both—could dull how fierce she looked in the bare afterglow. Fierce but soft, utterly untouchable despite the undeniable way she melted in my arms.

My wings gave a flick. The motion curled the edges inward, shrouding her body where she rested against me, offering her a quiet shelter she didn't even know was there. Her weight grounded me, warm and too close, leaving nothing—not battle, not rage, not reason—to distract me. It was just her. Her scent in the thick air, the tension still crawling sharp under my skin, and the knowledge of what had just passed between us.

Stars above, I was already failing.

My instincts snarled, wild and unrelenting, demanding more of her. Touch her again. Taste her again. Claim her utterly.

I stilled, forcing a sharp inhale into lungs still aching from exertion. The sulfur-tinged air clung to my ribs, its bitterness scratching at my throat. But it wasn't what filled me now. No, all I could taste was her—the maddening sweetness beneath the salt tang of her sweat, the wild scent of something citrus. It clung to my tongue, lingering like a punishable indulgence, and some reckless, bone-deep urge wanted to taste it again. To remind her of this bond in ways she couldn't ignore.

Not yet. That leash was tighter than want, though the edges frayed enough that my claws twitched at their cage. I couldn't give in, not while her body still hummed with exhaustion pressed into my chest.

Selene shifted against me. The small motion—so subtle yet intimate—tore across every frayed nerve. My grip tightened on her hip, my palm warm and calloused against the thin fabric of the shirt I'd scavenged from her pack. Her fingers stirred against my ribs, a soft twitch that shouldn't have tugged at something deep inside me. And yet ... I memorized her, almost unconsciously, with a sharpened focus I couldn't explain even to myself.

I wished she was lying naked against me, but no amount of lust could overcome the reality of our location, and we'd hastily pulled on clothes before collapsing beside one another.

Her exhaustion softened her edges, and for half a moment, her guard gave way to something gentler. Her brown lashes rested softly against her cheeks.

Her chest rose in steady rhythm beneath my hand. I dragged my gaze over the shape of her.

Sanity should've returned by now, except it hadn't. I'd crossed every boundary I had no right to touch ... and still, it wasn't enough. The heat pulling tight through me hadn't dulled; it didn't burn out the way it should have. If anything ... it burned sharper now. Hungrier.

Mine.

Mate.

It wasn't something quiet anymore. The word crawled red-hot through every breath, every nerve, an ache gnawing sharp at the center of my chest. I hadn't said it aloud. I didn't need to. Every time my fingers skimmed delicate bones beneath too-fragile skin, I came closer to losing the leash entirely.

She wasn't just mine. She was *her*—stubborn, maddeningly human, and so gorgeously unbreaking she made all of Volcaryth look brittle by comparison. No molten river could claim her, no volcanic ridge could match her stubborn, radiance. And she still didn't know, did she?

Selene tilted her head, a soft brush of her temple against the dip of my collarbone. Heat sparked, unbidden and familiar where her pulse beat. My throat locked around the need coiled there, wrapping tight through sinew and muscle. Every part of me wanted to take more—to feel *more*—but instead, my fingers eased into that moment.

I forced myself still. Anything less threatened whatever frayed balance I'd clawed back. The whisper of her name burned against my tongue, bitter smoke tight at the edges. If I'd let it slip now, if I'd told her—

Forge save me, I wanted to tell her.

If she saw everything unraveling in me now, she'd never believe it. The truth. That no ridge, no fault line, no uncharted piece of this godless terrain could break me half as easily as she could.

And if I wasn't careful ... she *would*.

"I can *feel* you thinking," Selene muttered, her voice soft and frayed at the edges, though laced with a bit of humor. Her hand nudged weakly at my chest—not a push, not even close, but strong enough to pull my focus back to her because of course she'd notice.

Of course *she* would find space to tease even now.

I blinked down at her, the corners of my mouth twitching despite myself. "You should be sleeping."

"So should you."

I tilted my head. "Are you fussing at me?"

My claws shifted against her hip, the motion careful, restrained. She didn't pull away. Didn't stiffen. But she did look up at me, eyes catching reflections of distant light. The glow carved firelight into her expression, pulling tight against every stubborn edge of her.

"You're impossible," she muttered. The softness beneath the words caught somewhere deeper—fragile, not from weakness, but from something she wouldn't offer easily.

"And you're still here," I replied.

Selene snorted, though the sound lacked edge. Fragile. Tirelessly human. The tension between us dulled—not into emptiness, but into something quieter. Something heavier. It settled there, like this volatile mountain ridge couldn't shift it.

Her head tilted, gaze slipping past me toward the expanse of Volcaryth unfolding just beyond the crumbled plateau. The landscape was vicious in its beauty, a sprawling labyrinth of broken black rock and shimmering heat. The rivers of lava threading veins deep into the mountains glowed, casting distorted shadows across her sharp features.

"What is this place to you?" she asked quietly, her voice tinged with something sincere enough to unbalance me.

I stilled.

My focus cut away from her face, following the long spires of dark peaks breaking against the stifling haze. Her tone was soft but unflinching, brushing against the edges of something I hadn't intended to acknowledge.

"It's a proving ground," I said finally. "There was a time when young Drakarn warriors who thought they'd finished their training came here. The Harrovan Mountains are cruel, but surviving them ..." My claws flexed against her side. "The ones who came back weren't just warriors anymore."

"It's different now," I continued. The weight tightened in my chest before I could stop it, rougher than the air clawing its way through the rocky expanse under us. "The terrain is too unstable. Fewer came back. And Ignarath has expanded their territory; we're not far from the border." My thumb moved along the curve of her waist. "They would not take kindly to this mission."

Her lips parted, not in argument, but with questions lining the space between us. She didn't ask them.

Her head shifted, brushing against my chin. I should have held her still, anchored her completely into this moment before her restless thoughts took her another direction. But I couldn't bring myself to do it—not when it was Selene, not when her fire kept breaking apart things I thought I'd buried long ago.

She settled back against me, and her soft, shallow breaths melted into an even sleep.

I sat there for awhile before finally, my own eyelids drooped, and I joined her in the peace of slumber.

Then it shattered.

A scream split the still air, and I jerked upright, looking for its source.

Vyne's growl vibrated through the stone beneath me just as a scream ripped through the air like shattering glass.

My mind scrambled to catch up as I jerked awake, muddled by the haze of sleep, but that scream —the shrill, fractured sound of it—dug hooks into my ribs and wrenched me into full awareness.

Burnt air clawed my throat, a rush of sulfur and steam making my lungs sting with each breath. Vyne was already moving, a shadow of coiled muscle and tension at my side.

I sat up too fast, nearly tangling myself in his wings as they flared wide. They blotted out what little morning light there was, stretching like shields over me while his claws flexed against the ground, nearly carving into the stone with the force of his restrained fury.

Another scream echoed, high and desperate. My stomach twisted.

That voice was human.

"Stay," Vyne growled, not looking at me. Just one word, clipped and commanding.

"Wait—" My arm shot out, but too late. He moved faster than I could keep up, his entire frame lifting into the air with a single beat of his wings. Wind whipped over me as his shadow disappeared into the sulfur mist hanging above.

My pulse thundered in my ears.

Stay? Seriously?

Not in this fucking lifetime.

The scream echoed again, and instincts I couldn't argue with shoved me upright.

The grip of fear clawed its way up my spine, but it was overrun by something heavier, louder. *Move.* My body, my muscles, every ounce of my awareness latched onto that need.

The ridges leading upward were unforgiving. Shards of volcanic rock scraped at my palms as I climbed, the grit slipping underneath my boots and threatening to spill me onto the unstable terrain below.

By the time I crested the ridge, I could barely think through the heat and the choking pressure in my chest. But my focus narrowed fast when I spotted the source of the chaos.

First, the woman. Ragged and trembling, trying to hold her ground even as her feet scraped against loose rubble edging toward a fissure. Her clothes were tattered, her bare arms streaked with grime, hair clinging to her sweat-soaked skin in uneven clumps.

She was human. There wasn't any mistaking that.

Then her pursuer. He was Drakarn. His scales shimmered red, shot through with golden under-tones. I didn't recognize him or the armor he was wearing. Was he one of the Drakarn from Ignarath that Vyne had mentioned?

He moved with almost lazy slowness, stalking toward her like the whole mountain belonged to him. And her? She was nothing to him but something breakable.

My heart, already pounding hard, lurched.

Far above them, the clash of wings and roaring snarls shattered the silence. Vyne. Locked midair with someone equally massive. Their bodies tangled into an overwhelming storm of claws and fangs that blurred beyond my ability to follow.

But it was the woman's scream—the sharp, splintered crack of it—that dragged all my attention back. Her legs wavered beneath her, inching across the ridge. And that red-scaled bastard? He took another step forward, his pupils fixed on her with something too cruel and calculated to ignore.

I moved before I could think.

The knife Vyne had given me felt too small, too light in my hand as I gripped it tight enough to turn my knuckles white. What I wouldn't give for a gun right now.

Fear buzzed under my skin, clashing against the instinctive pull roaring through me to *do something*. My pulse hammered loud in my ears, drowning out everything but the scrape of my boots over the rock.

I descended the ridge, staying low, moving fast against the unstable ground. Shifting grit slipped underfoot, rock scraping against my palms and knees every time I braced myself against a drop too steep for balance.

Ahead of me, the red Drakarn shifted his weight forward, wings twitching just enough to draw attention to the brutal size of his frame. He stalked toward the human. It wasn't a question *if* he was going to act, only *when*.

Another half-sob, half-choking sound wrenched its way out of the woman. She stumbled another inch backward, and her heel skidded dangerously close to the wide fissure cutting through the ridge.

Hot air hissed from steam vents near the cracks in the earth, the sound sharp and uneven enough to claw through my focus. My legs burned from the scramble, my breath coming too fast, flooding my lungs with sulfur-tainted air.

But there wasn't time for pain, for doubt.

When I dropped the last few feet from the ridge and shoved myself between them, the red-scaled Drakarn finally noticed me. His head shifted, eyes locking onto me with a predatory calm.

I raised the blade to level with his chest.

"Get back," I said, though the quaver in my voice betrayed something thinner than confidence.

The woman went still. Her breathing was still too loud, too ragged. I'd worry about that later.

The Drakarn drew in a breath through wide flared nostrils, his lips quirking upward enough to reveal serrated fangs.

"You're either brave," he drawled, voice dark and unnervingly smooth, "or stupid."

"Try me."

It wasn't my cleverest line, but my grip tightened around the knife all the same. The edge of its hilt dug sharp into my palm as I shifted closer, as steady as I could force myself to be.

The red-scaled bastard chuckled, low and sharp as breaking rock. It wasn't loud, but it hit heavy, curling out with enough force to vibrate through the ever-thinning space between us.

"Stand aside, human." He tilted his head slowly, his tail flicking behind him with a few unhurried snaps. "This one is mine."

"Not anymore." I took one step back. Far enough that he'd have to do more than swing lazily to reach me. For every inch I moved, though, it felt like I was sinking deeper into boiling water.

Behind me, I could feel her trembling. Her panic, her desperation, was a raw heat spilling into the space like the sulfuric air hissing dangerously from the nearest vents. She had to keep it together. If she made a break for it, there wasn't anything I could do.

The Drakarn's gaze burned, yellow and sharp, catching at the thin line of my knife like nothing more than child's play.

For a moment, I thought maybe—maybe—he'd say something else. Some drawn-out breath of mockery to give me the chance to step back, shut him down before this could escalate even further.

But no.

His whole body shifted instead, his weight rolling forward into one swift strike.

It came fast—too fast. The whip of his tail lashed through the air a half breath before his claws could follow, spiking against the loose rubble ahead of him as I barely threw myself back far enough to evade.

Heat stole the air from my lungs, pulling a searing gasp out of me as my boots scraped against stone, and the knife twisted forward on instinct alone.

The strike didn't land. He was faster, and his twisted grin made sure I knew it.

"Sloppy," the Drakarn taunted.

I couldn't waste time trading jibes with this beast, but it was everything standing between the woman and the narrowing sliver of rocky ridge left beneath us. I stepped forward again, blade steady, pulse anything but.

Come on, Vyne.

It was almost enough to keep him in place. Almost.

Then the sound hit.

The thump of a limp and heavy body crashing against unforgiving stone.

Then the roar.

Louder, more raw, deeper than my knife or his claw could have cut past.

It carried sharp across the ridge, rough and furious, breaking control of every sound or thought I'd tried to hold onto in the moment.

When Vyne came down from the air, it *wasn't* calculated, smooth, or finely executed as I'd come to expect from him. This wasn't control.

This was rage, and it hit with force enough to split the ridge wide beneath both Drakarn.

The red Drakarn bucked under Vyne's impact, claws scrabbling against crumbling rock as he reeled forward. His wings flared for balance, but Vyne didn't let him recover. Talons locked deep into his opponent's shoulders, ripping downward in a vicious arc that sent blood splattering across the ridge.

The clash was deafening—snarls and bone-rattling roars that echoed around us. Vyne's movements were sharp, relentless. Calculated violence gave way to unpredictability, and I caught the glint of his fangs as he lunged for the red-scaled warrior's throat.

Air rushed past me in dizzying bursts that stole my breath. The fight was too fast, too brutal—green and red scales blurred in and out of the sulfur haze rising from the heat vents.

This wasn't the Vyne I knew. His precision was still there, but it was wrapped in something unrestrained. Something that didn't stop for control or reason.

My chest tightened painfully as I forced myself closer to the woman. Her ragged breathing was practically a wheeze now, audible even above the hiss of steam and the crashing of claws on stone.

"I'm here," I managed, my voice sharp and strained as I crouched low. My knees pressed into the unstable rock, hands tightening around the knife until the metal cut cold into my palm. She flinched at the sound of my voice, her eyes cutting toward me in recognition before another tremor in the ground wrenched her focus away.

Above us, the battle whirled in unpredictable surges. Vyne struck fast—aiming for weak points with brutal efficiency—but the red-scaled warrior lashed out harder, the weight of his strikes threatening to overpower Vyne's speed.

A snap of wings. A hiss of claws. The silence of held breath before a tail cracked the air.

Vyne twisted mid-dodge, his wings beating downward in a ruthless push that drove his enemy farther back toward the ledge. His claws sliced clean along a vulnerable patch of scales near the other Drakarn's chest, and the snarl that erupted in response sent a spark of panic rocketing through me.

I couldn't look away. Couldn't even blink.

The red-scaled warrior lunged, his claws reaching wide with a force that could crush bone—

and barely missed. He stumbled under his own weight as Vyne rolled out of the way, dragging a second strike along the length of his enemy's exposed side.

Blood splattered the ridge in dark streaks.

It was violent. Brutal. Terrifying.

The woman whimpered again behind me, tearing my attention away just long enough to see how badly she was shaking. Her hands clutched at her sides, fingers pale and trembling, her chest rising and falling too fast as she gasped for air she couldn't seem to find.

"It's going to be okay," I said to her firmly, keeping my voice low and steady despite the nause- ating churn of dread in my stomach. "Just stay behind me. I've got you."

Her head jerked in what might have been a nod —hesitant, broken—but her weight shifted forward like she meant to try. She didn't say anything, her cracked lips trembling as her eyes darted between me and the fight above.

A hiss snapped my attention back to Vyne just in time to see the red-scaled warrior's body twisting unnaturally at the ridge's edge. A final swing—a desperate last strike—broke through Vyne's attempts to pin him fully down, and the larger Drakarn's wings flared wide as he slashed upward.

The blow grazed Vyne's wing, ripping through the delicate membrane as he snarled and pressed in harder.

Together, their weight sent a tremor crashing through the ridge as the unstable ground beneath them buckled again.

"Vyne!" I shouted, my voice sharp enough to cut over the volcanic hiss.

He didn't hear me—or if he did, his focus stayed locked entirely on his opponent.

His claws drove forward, ripping through the edges of armor-like scales and drawing a guttural, labored roar from the other Drakarn. Even through the blood, the snarling, and the unrelenting violence of the moment, Vyne's purpose rang clear.

He wasn't just fighting. He was finishing this.

The ridge groaned under their combined force, crumbling farther as the red-scaled warrior's claws lost their grip.

But as the fight tipped all its weight into the battle above, it left the ground beneath *me* wobbling too close to breaking.

Another fissure split through the stone just inches behind my heels, and I grabbed the woman's arm fast to pull us both back before the broken edge of the ridge could give way entirely.

Her hands clung tightly to my arm now, fingernails digging into my skin like she didn't trust her own legs to hold her upright anymore.

I caught her eyes again.

"Please," she begged softly, her voice cracking under the force of what should have been louder words. "Please, help me. Save me from these monsters."

I tightened my grip on the woman's arm as her knees faltered, pulling her upright as the unstable ground shifted beneath us. Tiny cracks webbed across the ridge, sulfuric steam hissing erratically through stone. One wrong step and we wouldn't just fall— we'd vanish into volcanic hell.

Her fingers clung to me like a lifeline, trembling so violently I thought she might hurt herself. She wasn't just scared—she was unraveling. Her breath came shallow and unsteady, each gasp sharp enough to punch holes in her control. But I didn't let go.

"Hey!" I snapped, keeping my voice low but firm. "Eyes on me. You're okay—I'm not going to let anything happen to you, alright? We're getting out of this."

A low, guttural roar erupted from higher up the

ridge, rattling the heat-laden air around us. The sound froze her, her whole body tensing as she flinched hard into my side. I didn't have to look to know where the fight was coming from. I trusted Vyne. I knew he wouldn't let the bastard get anywhere near us—but she didn't.

"It's okay," I murmured, shifting my grip so I could keep her closer, steadier. "I need you to breathe. Deep and slow. Focus on my voice."

Her whimper broke my momentum. It was a quiet, splintered sound full of something I recognized far too well—panic that didn't just come from this one moment. This wasn't fear of an immediate threat. This was someone who'd been living on edge for far too long, stripped bare by circumstance.

How was she here? There weren't supposed to be any humans on Volcaryth outside of my people back in Scalvaris. I wanted to ask, but she wasn't in any place to answer. Not yet.

"Come on. One step at a time. Don't look back." I spoke with layers of calm I didn't feel, keeping it steady as the adrenaline clawed at my chest.

She stumbled, legs folding mid-step. My arm shot out, snapping around her waist to keep her upright. She gasped, her breath hitting like broken glass, but she didn't try to resist when I steadied her again.

"Deep breaths," I said, a little softer now. "You're doing fine. Just keep your feet—steady now."

Her knuckles were bloodied, her fingers curling against me so tightly it felt like she'd carved grooves into my side. Too strong for her to be completely powerless, but too desperate for it to matter. She wasn't thinking anymore; she was surviving on raw instinct, and I had to be enough for both of us.

Every inch we covered rattled underfoot. Tiny fragments of volcanic stone scattered with each shifting step. The ground hissed beneath us, not quite stable but stable enough. I kept us moving, slow and steady, even when my muscles barked protest. There wasn't another choice—not if we wanted to live.

I let out a slow breath as the ridge sloped down-ward into smoother terrain. "Okay," I murmured, more to myself than her, though she clung tighter in response. "We're getting there. Just a little farther."

Her head shook, her response staggered and broken. "I ... didn't think anyone ..."

Her voice cracked into silence. Her whole body jolted against me when another echoing roar rippled through the air, closer this time.

Her trembling grew fiercer, her voice trembling loose again in barely audible fragments. "... anyone would come."

The words, slurred and barely there, hit somewhere I couldn't place. My jaw tightened. But this
wasn't the moment—not to process, not to dig
deeper. Her survival—*our* survival—had to come
first.

"You're not alone now," I told her plainly,
adjusting my grip as the incline leveled out into an
uneven path along the ridge's edge. My boots skidded, but I dug in to steady us both. "Keep moving.
We're almost there."

I could see the edge of the campsite past an
outcropping, and for the first time since we'd started
moving, relief crept into my chest.

Just a little farther. We could make it.

The ground leveled out beneath us just as her
knees gave way completely. She collapsed where she
stood, crumpling back against the blackened rock.
Her thin shoulders heaved with each gulp of air,
trembling as though even breathing was a battle she
wasn't sure she could win.

I crouched in front of her, keeping a firm hand
on her shoulder to hold her steady, grounded.
"You're safe," I told her, my own breath pushing hard
through my lungs. "Do you hear me? We're safe for
now. Breathe." A pause. "In through your nose—
slow. I need you to slow it down."

Her bloodshot eyes, wide and panicked, snapped

to mine. They searched me wildly as if looking for any crack in my composure that might justify her spiraling fear. I didn't give her one. I stayed rock-solid in front of her, forcing calm into my voice where my muscles only screamed for rest.

She nodded shakily and dragged an uneven breath through her nose. It hitched but didn't spiral right away. Promising. The next breath was a bit steadier, though still a far cry from ideal.

"Good," I said, my voice lowering into something soothing, steady. "Keep it up. You're okay—we're okay."

Even as I reassured her, I couldn't stop my clinical instincts from taking inventory. Up close, she was worse off than I'd realized. Deep bruises shadowed her skin, swelling and discoloration scattered unevenly between deep gashes and ugly scrapes. Her clothes were burnt and torn, as if she'd crawled out of the steam vents themselves.

Too thin. Ribs showing beneath her battered skin, her limbs trembling from both dehydration and exhaustion. She was a human-shaped survival instinct at this point, hurt and collapsed within herself, and still somehow breathing.

"What's your name?" I asked as I reached for my supply pack.

Her lips trembled, just shy of a reply. Then the

quietest whisper slipped through her cracked mouth. "Reika," she rasped, the word catching like shards in her throat.

"Reika," I repeated gently, giving her shoulder a reassuring squeeze. "Alright, Reika. I'm Selene. Nice to meet you." I unclipped the tiny water pouch from my kit, ignoring how worryingly little remained inside. "Here. Drink—but slow, alright? Don't push it too fast."

Her trembling hands reached out, faltering before brushing the pouch. For a split second, I thought it might drop between us, wasted completely. But she managed, gripping the edge with shaking fingers and raising it hesitantly to her lips. Her gaze stayed pinned on me the entire time, like she was waiting for me to snatch it back or slap it from her hands.

Small, steady sips left little trickles at her mouth's edge, but she didn't choke, didn't splutter.

"Good," I said. Her breaths came easier now— rough, yes, but better. "Alright, let's take a closer look at those cuts."

She didn't protest when I reached for her forearm. An ugly gash ran deep enough to graze muscle beneath her sunburned skin. I grabbed what supplies I could from the remains of my med kit, working quickly to clean it out.

"This one's going to sting," I warned her quietly. "Tell me if it hurts, and we can stop."

"Why ... why are you helping me?"

I paused and really looked at her. It wasn't suspicion I saw there. It wasn't anger or even gratitude. Just ... confusion. Unfiltered confusion that radiated like a wound of its own.

"Because you need it." The simplicity of my tone didn't waver as I resumed cleaning the wound. "I'm a medic. That's how this works."

Her silence spoke louder than anything else after that.

I finished wrapping her forearm, then moved lower to inspect the uneven swelling along one ankle. There were blisters there, crackling like ruptured masses across swollen flesh. The burns from running this volcanic hellscape were clear—painful and likely pricking at every nerve with hot rods of agony. She clenched her jaw tight as I lifted the ankle, saying nothing but letting out a sharp, unsteady exhale as I worked.

"Alright, I've got you," I murmured when her trembling turned harsher at one particularly deep press. "Stay with me. You'll be good as new in no time."

A weak scoff croaked out despite her pain—brief, edged with disbelief but still there. That was something. I gave her a short glance, arching my brow in mock challenge.

"Too soon for jokes," she rasped.

I shrugged, the corner of my mouth twitching into a hint of a smirk. "It beats screaming."

She blinked like she didn't know how to respond to that, and I turned my focus back to her injury. The bandages pulled tight against the weakened joint, stabilizing it enough. I couldn't promise miracles, but she'd survive. That was enough for now.

The beat of wings blew hot rock dust toward us. My pulse jumped, though not out of fear this time. I straightened, glancing behind me just as Vyne picked his landing spot across the wide edge of our makeshift perch.

The impressive slam of his claws against the charred rock sent tremors skittering along the stone. His bloodied scales caught the dim light, and there were brutal shadows around him. His scent made the air sharper, though it wasn't rage he carried back with him.

Reika stiffened to stone beside me.

"Shit," I cursed. Her head snapped toward Vyne, and her eyes exploded with panic. Every trace of calm dissolved before I could react further.

She screamed. Loud, wrenching, full of wretched terror that ripped the fragile silence apart.

Before I could think to restrain her, she scrambled blindly against the rough slope, dragging herself backward on bloodied palms and shaking arms.

"Reika!" My voice was sharp, a cutting force meant to ground her. "Stop! He's not going to hurt you."

Her panic swelled even more, animalistic and frantic, fueled by something deep and unrelenting. Her lips trembled, chest heaving violently. "M-monster!" she stuttered, though it fractured midway between a sob and a hiccup of air. "He's one of them! He's—he's—"

"Enough," Vyne's command thundered ahead of him, barbed and hard enough to shake the air itself. It hit like steel clashing against metal, his low growl carrying authority designed to break panic rather than stir it.

Reika froze completely. Her body locked, trembling harder now, on the perilous edge of total collapse.

I shifted between her and Vyne, one hand lightly pressed to her shoulder again as I murmured quiet reassurances. "You're safe. He's with me. He won't hurt you."

Vyne's glinting, yellow gaze burned sharp through the remnants of smoke between us—

controlled, restrained. After a long beat, he stepped back, his wings folding tight.

"You're hurt," he rumbled at me. His voice was low, tension radiating from every fiber of his frame.

"I'm fine. Bruised, maybe," I said quickly, brushing dust from my scratched forearms. I was too focused on Reika to think about my own pain.

When the silence stretched too long, I sighed, folding my arms across my chest to mask my wobbling exhaustion. "Seriously, Vyne. It's nothing."

"You've seen better days," he growled softly, moving closer with talon-scraping steps over the rock. His chin tipped down, eyes locking onto mine.

Reika hissed in a sharp breath and started to judder with fear. Her breaths came in fast. She was hyperventilating now.

If I couldn't calm her down, I had no idea what to do. We couldn't just leave her there.

"He's different from them. Trust me. I wouldn't bring a threat near you."

Her lips quivered, every line in her face clinging to disbelief like it was the only thing between her and oblivion. "You don't know," she whispered, broken and terrified. "You don't understand."

"Maybe not," I said softly, still holding her gaze. "Look at me, Reika. I know enough to bet my life on him. I need you to trust me, just for now. Believe me when I say you're safe with us."

Her breathing continued to hitch, but the trembling slowed a little, her muscles inching closer to unfrozen. She shuddered—not entirely convinced, but no longer drowning in pure terror.

"We need to leave," Vyne said. His eyes swept over both of us, lingering on Reika just a beat longer before cutting back to me. "More are coming. They'll smell their fallen before long, and when they do, they won't come alone."

I looked at Reika, her fragile state etched in the tight cords of her trembling frame. She'd stopped trying to crawl away, but her fear still radiated like heat, coiling tense and unrelenting. She wouldn't make it far on her own, and carrying her across the ridges would slow all three of us to a death sentence.

I didn't allow my focus to linger long before shifting it to Vyne. His massive wings, even folded tightly against his back, couldn't hide the damage stretching from the nasty tear along the edge. Blood seeped out with each twitch of his movements, though he held himself upright, impassive. His strength was undeniable—but strength had its limits, and his were closer than he let on.

He was hurting. She was barely holding on. And

all I could do was try to hold the weight of that in both hands without anyone slipping through.

"We need speed," Vyne said, bracing one shoulder against the rock as though the admission itself irritated him. "I can fly her ahead. There's a second ridge farther west—secluded enough to lose the Ignarath if we move quickly. She'll be safer there."

"No," Reika rasped, cutting him off violently before I could answer. Her voice cracked on the word, panic rising sharp as claws, latching onto any semblance of control she thought she could salvage. "No. You can't—you can't let him take me."

Her breath grew rough again, and she pressed herself harder into the rock, trembling visible anew. "He's just like them. I can't— I won't—" Her words stuttered, and she started shaking again.

"Reika," I interrupted, kneeling down and catching her frantic gaze before the spiral could fully consume her again. "Reika, listen to me. He's not like them. I need you to hear me."

She shook her head so hard I feared she might hurt her neck, her wide-eyed panic driving her further into denial. "You don't understand!"

"Then help me understand." My voice stayed firm—unshaking, despite exhaustion pressing cracks into my resolve. "Tell me what happened."

Her body jolted at the words, her gasp rough and staccato, but she stopped moving. Her trembling didn't vanish, but she stared at me now, not through me. Something in her wild gaze softened—or at least tolerated the possibility that my words weren't a trap.

I exhaled, gesturing between the three of us. "We don't have options right now. We can't win if more come. So, here's the question: are you willing to get out of here alive, or do you want to face the Ignarath again?"

She didn't answer. Her lips pressed thin and pale, punctuated with blood pricking at the cracks. Her eyes tipped downward—not toward rocky escape paths, not back toward Vyne.

After what felt like minutes compressed into seconds, she nodded—the smallest, reluctant tilt of her head. "No flying," she insisted.

I swallowed hard against the surge of frustration. Turning, I met Vyne's gaze. "We have to walk," I said, my tone final. "You need to rest your wing."

"You're too stubborn for your own good," he muttered, more to himself than me. But he didn't argue. That told me how much his wing had to be hurting.

He took a careful step back, giving Reika space to breathe even as his presence still filled the ridge's confined air. And with that same controlled precision, he angled closer to me, his body a fortress of heat and vigilance.

"She won't keep pace long," he warned, though his tone had softened by now. "If her strength fails—"

"It won't," I said, cutting him off. The conviction in my voice tasted stubborn even to myself. "We'll figure it out."

I turned back toward Reika and extended a hand once more. She hesitated just a fraction before gripping it shakily and standing.

I hitched my pack over my shoulder and tried not to think of the vyrathis inside as Vyne led the way down a narrow path.

I scanned the path ahead, blinking only when the sting of sulfur forced it. Wind shifted around us in thin, sharp currents—too erratic for comfort, too quiet for complete safety. We had to keep moving.

Behind me, Selene murmured softly, voice calm and almost stern. "Just breathe through it, Reika. A few more steps. We'll rest soon."

Selene moved with no hint of hesitation, her focus so tightly woven into tending to the fallen woman it was as though the volcanic landscape didn't even exist.

And, stars above, it wrecked me.

Selene should've been the one resting. Her temples glistened with sweat, smudged with streaks of soot she either hadn't noticed or hadn't cared to wipe away. Scratches scored her exposed skin in uneven patterns.

She deserved better than this journey. Better than this ridge.

Better than me.

She slowed, giving Reika another of those delicate touches—her fingers ghosting over the woman's trembling wrist in a silent reassurance only she could make believable. I exhaled and turned my focus forward again.

It was safer to study the path. Safer not to let myself get dragged under whatever storm she stirred in me: longing, hunger, something deeper I couldn't name without risking it breaking loose.

Selene's tone turned teasing despite her heavy burden. "Eyes up. The rocks are more afraid of you than you are of them."

Reika's clipped response was little more than a broken grunt. Progress, of sorts—she wasn't screaming or cowering anymore. I'd lost count of how many times the woman had locked up mid-stride, her terror bracing through even the smallest glance in my direction.

Her gaze hadn't met mine for longer than a heartbeat since Selene had convinced her to move. But she *was* moving, and that was what mattered.

But more than that ... Selene wouldn't let her break further. Her boundless, maddening kindness wouldn't let her. And something in me knew better than to pretend I didn't admire that.

Maddening. Beautiful. *Mine.*

Control coiled its leash tight through my ribs again, its strain aching. I rolled my shoulders briefly, peeling the tension out in careful movements as my claws flexed against my sides.

"We need to stop." Selene's attention lifted toward me. "I need to clean her cuts before they get worse."

I fought to keep my voice steady. "Stopping too long is a risk. If the Ignarath come back over this—"

"Don't start with me." Her tone cut sharply, then dipped lower when I turned. "We need fifteen minutes."

I swallowed back a sharp retort, releasing a low growl instead. My wings snapped out for a brief stretch, and I winced at the ache. "We can spare five."

Her jaw twitched, but she nodded.

The moment I stopped moving, the pain caught up like a rival who'd been waiting for their chance to strike. My wing burned in gnawing pulses I could feel down to the bone. It was the kind of pain you could bargain with—if you didn't mind bleeding through every demand.

The tear wasn't deep, but every shift turned the injury into a throbbing reminder of my limits. I flexed my shoulder experimentally, keeping my wings tight against my frame. No use letting Selene catch the tremble as my body betrayed me. Not that she'd miss it for long.

Behind me, her voice was soft and low, pulling some semblance of calm from Reika's frantic breaths. Watching Selene ease the woman out of panic was almost worse than the pain—each word weaving that impossible warmth into this barren land, each steady hand doing what my claws never could.

I clenched my jaw and turned my focus forward, scanning past the darkening shadows of the ridges cutting against the hazy horizon. Volcaryth was unforgiving in its silence, but no fresh tremors rattled beneath us. No sulfur-drenched breeze tipped me off to Ignarath warriors cutting through the paths we'd left behind.

We'd crossed the edge of their claimed territory and were safe.

For now. But we had to keep moving.

Rest time was over.

We walked for over an hour before Selene's voice

drifted over. "Vyne." One word, carrying the weight of so many unsaid.

I glanced over at her. There she was, crouched beside Reika, her hands steady.

Her tone turned firm, leaving no room for refusal. "She can't go much farther. We need to make camp."

My claws flexed in resignation. "Soon." The word came out clipped, more at myself than her. Her lips twitched in fleeting triumph, though her gaze stayed heavy.

"Good."

I dropped to a crouch. The sharp pulse of pain still pounded steadily when I tucked them tighter, but nothing quieted the deeper pressure buzzing beneath it.

The outcropping up ahead wasn't much, but it was enough. Stone walls jutted between us and the open ridgeline, creating a half-shelter tucked against the mountain's angry edges. No overhead cover to hide us from any Ignarath scouting aerial paths, but it kept the worst of the sulfurous winds at bay.

It would have to do.

Selene already had Reika settled near the base of one wall, propping her up with a pile of shredded fabric pushed under her head like a pillow. Her improvised med kit lay scattered across the ground.

Reika's breaths came shallow and uneven, and her eyes fluttered closed against the world. Exhaustion had overtaken her panic for now. That alone did more for our chances of survival than any words I might have offered.

Selene's head turned toward me, sharp and direct—an acknowledgment, not an invitation. Her hands stayed carefully busy, adjusting the thin strips of bandage around Reika's bruised wrists. The movements were methodical, practiced.

"Selene." Her name tasted unfamiliar on my tongue, drawing something gentler out of me. "Enough. She's fine."

For once, she didn't argue. She breathed out, shoulders sinking. I wasn't sure if it was exhaustion or agreement, but it didn't matter.

Instead, she shifted subtly toward me, propping her back against the same slope of rough stone wall. Her hair fell loose over one shoulder. Without the distraction of motion, sharp exhaustion shadowed every inch of her.

"Let me see your wing." Her tone was low but pointed.

I stilled, my own exhaustion heavy enough to blur the words before they sank in. "It's nothing," I countered too quickly. Vainly.

Her hand nudged toward my arm, not with force

but with enough weight to slice through my half-hearted response. Her touch was light, but the slow trace of her fingertips across my wing struck deeper than her sharpest arguments ever had.

"I told you—" The words dissolved when her fingers pressed gently against the torn edge of skin along the membrane. My thoughts scattered in an instant, as though her lightest touch had broken them on purpose.

Her fingers withdrew in one swift, careful motion. "You'll live."

My own hand lingered just beside hers without thought—brushing lightly against the edge of her wrist.

It wasn't enough.

It wasn't ever going to be enough.

I settled against the rock, muscles tight despite the attempt to rest. Selene leaned into my side without hesitation.

Her breathing was steady now, slower than before but still weighed down by exhaustion. The tension in her frame hinted at an ache she refused to let show. Even now, when her body craved rest, her thoughts cut through the thick silence between us. I didn't need to read her mind to know she was thinking of a dozen questions she wouldn't voice, not yet.

She broke the haze of heat and silence with a pointed question. "How long will it take us to reach Scalvaris on foot?"

I turned my head. Her hair was still mussed, half sticking to her temple in damp streaks, but her eyes never wavered. Stubborn, focused, and entirely unyielding.

"A week." The subtle twitch in my wing flared as if protesting. "Maybe more, depending on how far west we must go to avoid Ignarath patrols."

Her lips parted to argue—or worse, suggest something reckless—so I cut her off. "Don't even think about it." My words came out in a low growl. "If you're about to suggest I fly ahead to deliver the vyrathis, forget it. I'm not leaving you out here alone, in enemy territory, for days."

Her brows furrowed, annoyance flickering bright for a heartbeat before she sighed. "I wasn't going to say that." Her tone remained low. "I figured out three hours ago that you'd say no."

I huffed a quiet laugh, shifting my weight to adjust the angle of my aching wing. "You're learning, *Zhyvarin*."

That earned me a weak glare, but she let it drop. Instead, her eyes flicked briefly toward Reika, who lay asleep—or unconscious—on the uneven ground not far from us. The soft rise and fall of her chest barely betrayed she was still with us.

"I know the healers need the vyrathis, but we can't abandon Reika. Not like this. What do you think they did to her?"

"I don't know." My attention flicked to the fragile human shape crumpled against the stone. "Ignarath aren't kind to outsiders."

The weight behind her silence was heavy. I didn't look at her; I didn't need to. Her emotions were loud, even when she buried them behind reason. "And Scalvaris is so friendly?" The bitter humor in her voice was muted but still sharp enough to hit.

I laughed. "Compared to the Ignarath? Yes."

She blinked, as if genuinely startled by that response, and for a fleeting moment, her eyes shifted toward the landscape beyond the narrow ridge.

Her voice lowered. "Do you think she was on our ship? Is it possible there are more humans on Volcaryth? That they survived?"

She would know better than me. There were ancient stories of people from far away planets woven through our history, but I had never given them much thought until Selene and her fellow humans had crashed into the burning sands outside the city.

"You'll have to ask her."

Selene didn't respond. I watched her in stillness, torn between wanting to do something—anything— to ease the weight she carried and the impossibility of action. Despite the razor edge of the situation, she still glowed. Stubborn as ever.

Mine, whether she knew it or not.

We were close now, both of us leaning against the walls that formed our makeshift camp. Her shoulder brushed mine—barely, but enough for my mind to fixate on it. Exhaustion should have dulled my senses, but no. The awareness of her warmth so near, the scent that clung to her as though even Volcaryth's heat couldn't burn it away.

I looked at her again, unable to help myself. Her profile was drawn in dimming light and shadow, and none of it was diminished by the grime and exhaustion streaked across her features. No, this was Selene at her rawest: worn but unbreaking.

And gods help me, I wanted her. Every stubborn, infuriating, breathtaking part of her.

I reached up and brushed a strand of her dark hair back, freeing it from where it clung to her temple. My knuckles grazed her skin—warm, impossibly soft against the sharp edges of this volcanic hellscape.

Her breathing hitched, just a bit, as her gaze darted to mine. She didn't pull away.

"*Zhyvarin*." Her mating name settled rough and reverent on my tongue.

Slowly, carefully, I tilted her face toward mine, my clawed thumb brushing her jawline with cautious precision. Her skin was fire beneath my touch—fragile and fierce all at once.

I leaned down, the world narrowing to the maddening slice of space between us. When my lips brushed hers, it wasn't with urgency. No battle raged in that moment, no ferocity vying for control. The kiss was slow, soft but consuming, a quiet clash of heat and restraint. Her lips trembled against mine before she leaned in, her entire frame pressing closer with painstaking grace.

I could have drowned in that.

Her hands found their way to my chest, resting lightly against the scales just above my heart. I felt her hesitation—not because she didn't want this, but because she did. Just as much as I did, perhaps more. The truth lingered between us, fragile and undeniable: there was no turning back from this.

And gods, for a moment, I didn't want to.

But then she pulled away, her forehead resting lightly against mine as her breaths came shallow and quick. The space between us lingered, crackling with unspoken intensity neither of us dared to tip farther toward.

"We can't." Her whisper broke the hush, voice heavy but steady.

My claws curled into my palms to keep my composure. "I know." The admission tasted like ash. "You should rest. I'll take first watch."

It was going to be a long night.

Reika trudged beside me. Her trembling had eased enough to keep her upright, though exhaustion clung to her shoulders like dead weight. Every step she took was driven by sheer will.

The strap of my pack cut into my shoulder, the clinking of the vyrathis container a reminder of what this delay could cost.

"How did you end up on Volcaryth?" I asked, keeping my voice low. If I'd been any less exhausted, I might have spent the night tossing and turning, desperate for the answer. Instead, I'd slept only a foot away from Vyne and wished I was brave enough to lie down in his arms.

This thing between us ... I wasn't sure I understood it. I could practically still taste him, the memory of his tongue a brand on me.

And I couldn't think about it. Not now, not when I had to keep Reika alive and get the vyrathis back to Scalvaris before it was too late.

Reika didn't respond. Not surprising—she still flinched whenever I said her name. Her gaze flicked toward Vyne's shadow ahead of us before her jaw clenched and she refocused on her uneven footing.

I tried again. "Were you on a generation ship from Earth? Maybe your pod got ejected somehow?" As best we could tell, that was what had happened to me and my fellow humans.

Her voice cracked when she finally spoke. "Does it matter?"

"It might," I said. "If there are others out there, they might need help."

She stopped. For a moment, I thought she'd stay silent, but then her lips curled into a sneer, her voice sharp and bitter. "If anyone else made it, you won't find them alive. You'd be lucky to find their bones."

The edge of her bitterness grated, but I swallowed my irritation. Pushing her wouldn't help, not while she was still bruised and battered. What the hell had she survived to leave her this cut open and closed off?

"What about you?" I pressed. "How long have you been out here?"

She didn't flinch this time. "Long enough."

She wore her silence like armor. And whatever survival instinct had dragged her through this volcanic deathtrap still burned under her exhaustion, just enough to keep her moving.

The terrain didn't help. The deeper we pushed into this wasteland, the more Volcaryth's suffocating hostility seeped into my bones. This world wasn't just a planet—it was a predator. Every shadow, every sulfur-choked breath in the air felt like it was waiting for one moment of weakness to strike.

Vyne moved steadily ahead. He knew the terrain better than either of us, but even he couldn't fully hide the tension. He saw something there—felt it.

He's worried.

That thought stuck to me harder than the heat. If Volcaryth had Vyne watching the shadows, we were already treading over the edge of disaster.

Reika kept moving, her steps growing steadier. Her breathing, still labored, was getting stronger. Whatever strength had dragged her through hell planet still burned inside her, faint but alive.

Then the first warning hit—a shift in the air, enough to make every nerve in my body tighten.

"Move." Vyne's voice cut like a knife.

Instinct took over before my mind could catch up. I shifted fast, dragging Reika toward me as I adjusted the pack against my back. My gaze darted upward to the surrounding ridges, searching desperately for whatever had Vyne's wings flaring.

Nothing. At least, nothing I could see.

"Eyes up," Vyne growled, his gaze locked on the rocks above. He stopped short, his imposing frame coiled and ready.

Then I saw them—shadows slipping over the peaks, moving too quickly and too precisely to be anything but a threat.

Shit.

"Reika." I kept my voice sharp and low, stepping closer to shield her as I reached for my knife. Vyne's knife. Whichever. All that mattered was it was sharp. "Stay close. Keep moving. Understand?"

She nodded stiffly, her breaths shaky but steady enough to keep her upright. Good. That was good. I could work with that.

The air thickened, tension coiling around us. It prickled behind my neck, each heartbeat louder and harder against my chest.

Then they appeared.

The first Drakarn, they had to be from Ignarath, burst from the haze, red and gold scales glinting. He slammed into the ground, his claws scraping deep gouges into the ridge just meters from Vyne. His wings flared sharply as he straightened.

A second leapt forward from the ridge to our left,

blue-scaled and bristling with dark armor so polished it seemed to drink in the shadows. Above us, a third circled.

"Stay behind me," Vyne growled. His body coiled, every muscle taut and ready.

I didn't argue. There wasn't time. Instead, I eased my stance, gripping the knife tighter in one hand while keeping my pack secured against my back with the other.

The first Ignarath launched himself at Vyne, claws outstretched. Vyne met him head-on, his strike brutal and precise, claws tearing at scales with surgical precision. Their impact echoed off the rocks, shaking the ground beneath me.

But as I tracked their fight, movement from the second Ignarath snapped my focus back. His eyes locked onto me. My stomach tightened. Big. Fast. Dangerous.

He lunged.

I dove low, heart hammering as his claws swiped just over my head. My blade sliced upward as I turned, grazing his flank. He let out a sharp snarl, twisting quickly to face me again. He was angry now —his tail snapping violently behind him, his gaze predatory and locked.

He swiped again, claws fast. I twisted, throwing awkward steps backward, barely keeping ahead of his momentum. Each move scratched away at whatever sandpaper-thin margin of survival I had left.

Focus. Keep moving.

His claws slashed wide, too fast for me to dodge. I threw myself sideways, the motion wrenching at my shoulders and sending me skidding on loose volcanic rock. Pain flared sharp along my ribs as I found my footing.

The bastard in front of me lunged again, claws slashing. I ducked, my knees scraping rock as I drove my blade upward. The edge of his wing caught my knife, tearing webbing and sending him reeling back with a guttural snarl.

The Ignarath growled. He was gauging me now —he hadn't expected resistance. His arrogance was personal. If I could exploit it, even for a moment ...

Footsteps.

No—pounding claws. Heavy, fast, closing in.

I turned sharply to see the second Ignarath, the blue-scaled brute, barreling toward Reika. Her scream sliced the air just as he reached her, his fangs bared and gaze alight with cruel intention.

Damn it.

"Reika!" I yelled, my heart slamming into my ribs. My body reacted, moving before my thoughts could catch up, muscles burning as I sprinted toward her. She was defenseless, frozen. I—

No. She wasn't.

She gripped a wickedly sharp piece of volcanic rock, her hands trembling. Her wide, panic-stricken gaze locked on the blue-scaled Ignarath, but there was a shift in the air. A thread of something wild sparked in her movements, shaky but there. Her terror turned sharp, desperate—but not paralyzed.

As his claws reached for her, Reika lashed out with the shard, the wide swing catching him clean across his forearm. Dark blood sprayed hot and fast against the stone, and the Ignarath's snarl turned to a roar of pain.

"Reika, get down!" I barked. She stumbled backward, the shard still clutched in white-knuckled hands.

The Ignarath recoiled, his fury radiating off him in near-tangible waves. He swiped again, and I barely had time to react, my body twisting sharply as he crashed into the ridge beside us.

My hands tightened around my knife as I maneuvered between Reika and the advancing Ignarath.

Fight. Survive. Protect.

That was all I could focus on now.

The Ignarath stalked closer, slow and steady now. He knew I was trapped. I could see it in the sharp curl of his lips, the evil grin that split his scaled face. His claws flexed, mocking, as if savoring the kill before he delivered it.

We were losing ground fast. I glanced past the Ignarath, trying to track Vyne, but I couldn't see him. The Ignarath snarled, his hand snapping out. A claw skimmed over my shoulder—not enough to tear flesh, but close enough to send me stumbling. Pain shot down my arm.

The bastard wasn't letting up. His massive wings folded to gain tighter control as his claws flexed and struck again. This time, I couldn't dodge fast enough. His hand clipped the side of my pack, dragging the weight of it hard against my ribs and knocking the air from my lungs.

The ridge around us felt alive—unstable rock shifting and groaning beneath the pressure of his sheer brutal force. My footing wavered as I stumbled farther back, the fissures widening behind me. He followed every step with relentless precision, cutting off any paths of escape with calculated strikes. This close, his size was overwhelming, his shadow swallowing the light as he pressed forward.

I just needed an opening. Anything.

A sharper sound cut through the air above us—a sudden rush of air displaced by powerful wings. My pulse kicked hard as I shifted my focus upward to the hulking shadow descending fast from above.

The third Ignarath hit the ground behind the first with a force that felt like an earthquake.

This one was broader, darker, his scales nearly black. His massive frame loomed, unnatural in its size and weight. His eyes burned, piercing gold—locking instantly on me, his wings still tucked tight against his back, claws flexing as he moved closer.

No hesitation. No slow circling this time. They weren't waiting anymore.

The weight of everything hit like a punch. My breath felt heavy and raw as my hand trembled harder around the knife hilt.

Vyne's roar broke through. I whipped my head toward him just as the emerald flash of his scales collided brutally with the first Ignarath. His claws tore into his opponent, forcing him toward the edge of the ridge. The fight was blood-slick and loud.

He didn't pause—didn't falter. Even with his wings frayed and blood streaking his sides, Vyne dominated the fight. But there were too many of them, and for every advantage he gained, it only pushed me harder into the realization:

He wasn't going to hold for long.

They weren't there to test our limits. They were there to tear them apart.

TWENTY
SELENE

My knife was too small against the sheer size of the Ignarath warrior in front of me. No time to second-guess; no time to think. Just react.

He circled closer, a predator toying with its prey. Claws sliced the hot, sulfurous air. Behind me, Reika's breaths were panicked gasps that clawed at my focus. I couldn't afford to look back, not even for a second. One wrong move, one glance away, and this bastard would gut me.

The Ignarath tilted his massive head, his slitted eyes narrowing in what I could only interpret as cruel amusement. "I will suck the marrow from your bones."

Great. He was going to enjoy this. Mockery on top of the very real threat of murder. The crimson streaks across his wings shimmered in the light, like hell's own tapestry come to life and intent on killing me.

This was bad. Beyond bad. Vyne was battling two of them now, his snarls and the sickening clash of talons echoing off the rocks. I tasted the metallic tang of fear on my tongue. How much longer could I keep this up?

Reika choked out a gasp, a fragmented attempt at a warning. I was too slow to process it, her voice splintered and lost in the fight, and that was all it took.

His claws lashed out, catching the strap of my pack and yanking me violently off-balance. I stumbled, one knee cracking hard against the hard stone. Pain exploded through my leg, white-hot and blinding. I swore and barely managed to throw my knife up in a useless defense as he bore down on me.

He came in again, faster this time, claws aimed with deadly precision straight at my chest. I braced uselessly, knowing this was it.

A wave of regret washed over me. Thinking of what could have been, all the things I wanted, this was the last thing I should be doing. But for a second, all I could think of was the taste of Vyne's lips against my own, of the way his body melded with mine. Of the creeping suspicion that there was something more, something *bigger* between us.

Or there would have been. If we had a chance at a future.

I'm sorry, Vyne.

But the blow never came.

The world shifted in a heartbeat. A thunderous slam echoed off the rocky walls as another massive figure collided with the Ignarath like a living firestorm of muscle and fury. The force of it sent shockwaves through the ground, knocking the crimson-scaled bastard back on his heels, his claws skidding uselessly against the stone as he scrambled to regain his footing.

Granite-gray scales gleamed as he straightened, his massive frame a nightmare—for my enemy, at least. For me? Relief flooded in, a surge of desperate strength.

I recognized this warrior.

Khorlar.

He didn't spare me so much as a glance. His narrow eyes burned only for the Ignarath in front of him, his jaw set, a terrifying stillness about him. It was clear: his next move was already decided, and it wouldn't end well for whoever stood in his path.

The Ignarath snarled, his wings flaring as he prepared to strike again. But Khorlar was faster, a blur of motion. He lunged forward with brutal effi-

ciency, his claws burying themselves with a sickening, wet crunch into the Ignarath's shoulder.

The bastard roared, a guttural, enraged sound
that was abruptly cut off when Khorlar's other hand
slammed hard into his ribs with the force of a
battering ram. The blow sent the Ignarath crashing
against the blackened rock wall, fissures spiderweb-
bing out from the point of impact.

It was over before I could fully react. Precise,
devastating strikes. He wasn't just fighting—he was
dismantling his opponent, piece by piece. There was
a terrifying economy to his movements, a cold, calculated brutality that left no room for doubt.

Above us, the shadow of the third Ignarath
loomed closer, circling lower with clipped strokes of
his massive wings. I swore under my breath. There
was no way even Khorlar, as powerful as he was,
could hold both of them off.

Vyne's opponent was backing off, shredded
scales a testament to Vyne's vicious efficiency—but
he was bleeding too, favoring one side. Exhaustion
was clear in every movement.

Another growl, closer this time, pulled my attention back down to Khorlar. He had already turned
his focus on the second Ignarath. I started to move
forward, ready to throw myself into the fray—stupid

or not, I couldn't just stand there—but the granite wall of a warrior didn't need my help.

Khorlar stepped into the attack. He ducked low under a sloppy, rage-fueled swipe, then drove his fist upward with explosive force into the Ignarath's exposed underbelly. The sound that followed was visceral, sickening—the crunch of scaled flesh and bone against the impact of volcanic strength. I winced, despite myself.

The blue Ignarath stumbled back, a mangled roar tearing from his throat, his wings twitching spasmodically as he jerked upward in a desperate attempt to retreat. Blood marred his once-pristine scales, leaving crimson streaks dripping in his wake, the volcanic air carrying the acrid scent of his pain and labored breathing before it all faded into the relative silence.

The ridge stilled.

I stayed frozen where I stood, my knife still clutched tightly in one hand, every nerve screaming for me to act, to react, to *do* something. But there was nothing left to do. The Ignarath were gone—either dead or retreating—and we were, miraculously, still alive.

Vyne landed behind me with a heavy thud, the turbulence of his wings stirring up a cloud of ash and dust around our feet. His breathing was steady, if strained, but I could see the tightness in his jaw, the almost imperceptible stiffness in the set of his shoulders. He was injured, no question, though he didn't give me a moment to ask, to assess.

"Hurt?" His voice was sharp, his concern settling on me. His gaze swept me from head to toe, his eyes narrowing when they caught on the shallow cut along my arm and the way my chest still heaved with exertion, each breath a ragged reminder of how close we'd come.

"I'm fine," I said quickly, waving off his concern with a dismissive flick of my wrist as I swiped the back of my hand across my dirt-streaked brow. "Nothing a shower wouldn't fix. What about you?" I needed to know, needed to see for myself. I wanted to throw myself at him, wrap my arms around him and never let go.

This thing between us was more than just lust. If I had more than a second to think about it, I might even call it ... No. There was no time. Not now.

Fuck it. I reached out and brushed my fingers against his arms, that little contact all I could allow, one little point of contact all there was to assure me he was still there, still alive.

It wasn't enough.

I wasn't sure if I imagined him leaning into my touch for just a second.

"Not relevant." He shifted his focus, his gaze moving to Reika, who had pressed herself as far back into the nearest rock wall as she could get, her bruised and battered frame trembling in the after-math. Her wide eyes flicked frantically between me, Vyne, and Khorlar, as though she couldn't decide which of us was the bigger threat.

"Reika." My voice softened, my knife slipping back into its sheath with a practiced flick. I crouched down near her, careful to keep my movements slow and non-threatening. "Hey. You okay? It's over. We're alright." *For now.* I kept the last bit to myself.

She didn't respond at first, her gaze locked on Khorlar with an intensity that spoke volumes. He still stood silently amidst the wreckage, a stoic, unmoving sentinel, radiating an aura of contained power.

Slowly, her trembling fingers loosened their death grip on the shard of volcanic glass she still clutched. Her breathing hitched, then steadied, her arms dropping heavily into her lap as if the weight of them had suddenly become too much to bear.

I exhaled heavily, a slow release of tension that had been mounting up throughout the fight—hell, ever since we'd left Scalvaris. Progress, even if she wasn't going to accept it yet.

Khorlar's raspy voice, devoid of any emotion,

finally broke the heavy silence that had settled over us. "There'll be more. We need to move."

He was right, of course. If their scouts didn't report back, reinforcements would follow. And they would be even more determined, more cruel.

Vyne was a steadying force despite the lingering adrenaline still crackling through my system. "We can't keep going like we have," he said, his gaze flicking between Reika and me, calculating. "We need to fly."

Reika stiffened immediately, her head snapping up to meet my gaze, a flicker of renewed panic in her eyes. "No," she croaked, the sound small and broken, filled with a deep-seated terror. "He'll ... he'll drop me. He'll hurt me. He'll—"

I was about to give her reassurances that I had no way of backing up when Khorlar came up to kneel in front of her. He held out a clawed hand. "I swear on my life you will be safe." His voice was rumbly. "I have never once dropped someone. I will not today."

I thought she might scream, might cower. She looked at Khorlar like he might grow a second head. She blinked rapidly, her chest heaving with shallow, unsteady breaths. For a long, agonizing moment, I thought her fear would win. But then, her lips parted, and a soft, wavering, "Okay," escaped.

Thank you, universe, for small favors.

It took longer than I'd have liked to coax her away from the relative safety of the wall, but eventually, she moved closer, her steps stiff and reluctant, carrying her toward Khorlar.

He growled softly, a low rumble, his wings tilting as he crouched down to better position Reika against his broad, scaled frame. Her trembling hands clutched at his arms, her knuckles white as she adjusted to the unfamiliar sensation of being supported, of trusting a Drakarn.

With a powerful thrust of his legs, Khorlar launched himself into the air.

I stepped into Vyne's arms, and he did the same.

TWENTY-ONE
VYNE

High canyon walls concealed our resting place from above, but the narrow space would trap us if anyone tracked us on foot. The air was too still, too oppressive. A warning.

Khorlar settled Reika against a concave fold near the canyon's edge, the shadows of burnt stone forming an uncertain cradle around her. She slept fitfully, the day's strain having gutted what little strength remained. Khorlar sat sentinel beside her, his massive frame an immovable barrier.

It was a good position—secure enough to rest, with clear visibility for watching the canyon's labyrinthine offshoots. The kind of place that would have let me relax, once—before all of this.

Before her.

Selene moved ahead, careful and sure on the

uneven ground. The strap of her pack dug into her shoulder, and her jaw ticked with tension. She wouldn't complain. Not aloud. But I saw.

She set the bag down but stared at it for a long moment, like she was worried it might disappear. After how far we'd come to get it, I could understand.

I approached her, my hands itching to touch, but I could feel Khorlar's watchful eye. We needed privacy, needed a moment alone. "The canyon's clear for now. Let's find a place to bed down. Khorlar has the girl and first watch."

Selene eyed me, more intuitive than I was prepared for. She studied me like she was calculating angles, risks, vulnerabilities—not from our enemies. Mine.

"Is something wrong with right here?" she asked.

I took the opening. "My side is bothering me." The admission was clunky, but her focus snapped immediately to me.

Healer's instincts—merciful and maddening.

"Why didn't you say something sooner?"

I blew out a breath and gestured toward a side passage just ahead. The fissure was painted in an uneven glow by some mysterious reflection of the suns. "It's nothing serious."

Selene didn't respond. Words weren't necessary;

her expression had already shifted to a mask of calm authority.

She followed me down the offshoot, small enough to force us to flatten against the warm stone to fit through. She didn't complain, her lips a tight line as the space opened ahead of us—a shallow alcove carved into the volcanic rock, hidden well beneath the canyon's natural shadows. Safe enough. For now.

And private.

I had to hide my grin.

"Alright," she said, dropping her pack with a muffled clink as tension cracked loose from her shoulders. She turned toward me. "Sit."

I arched a brow.

She bristled. "I mean it, Vyne. Let me see."

Shaking my head, I lowered myself onto a curved outcropping of stone and let my wings flare for balance. The warmth of the rock pressed into me, soothing muscles I wouldn't admit were aching. Her eyes flicked toward the way I held my arm against my ribs, how my wing shifted stiffly.

"Where does it hurt?" she demanded.

I flexed my arm, tilting to expose the stretch near my armpit—the shallow line of torn scales where the edge of an Ignarath talon had glanced me. The graze wasn't deep, barely more than a persistent sting and a sticky patch of dried blood. A minor wound. Negligible.

For Selene? It may as well have been catastrophic.

She sucked in a harsh breath. "Why didn't you tell me?"

"Because it wasn't relevant," I murmured, watching her.

"You're bleeding," she said flatly, daring me to argue.

"Not badly."

She huffed, pulling a small pouch from her belt. "Not the point."

The unexpected sting of her fingers brushing near the wound rattled something in me, and not from pain. She was so careful it hurt—like she assumed I'd break apart under her touch.

"It's not bad," I said at the growing line of panic in her frown. "Stop worrying."

Her lips thinned into a line as she continued, a damp cloth already pulling the stickiness of blood away from the torn scales. "Worrying's part of the job," she shot back, voice tight. "Especially when wounded warriors decide they're too tough to tell anyone about their injuries."

I almost laughed. Survival instincts choked it back.

When she finally pulled a roll of bandages from her kit, I caught her wrist lightly, fingers grazing the soft edges of her pulse. She froze, her gaze snapping to me.

"Selene." My voice dropped low, her name heavier this time. "It's nothing."

Her eyes held mine longer than they should have. The air thinned. For a brief flicker of time, the weight of the rock around us didn't press quite so hard. There was only her—brilliant, stubborn, impossible.

And, gods help me, mine.

But I let go, forcing the tips of my claws to unhook one by one. She kept watching me for a moment longer before dropping her gaze, her hands moving mechanically now as she wrapped the bandage. The heat of her fingers barely touched me. It wasn't enough.

"Done," she said, brushing residual dust from her palms and stepping back. "You should have told me sooner. What if you'd weakened during—"

"What? The flight?" I interrupted. "I would never drop you."

"You don't know that." Her tone was frustrated, her teeth worrying at her lower lip. This wasn't only a medic's training resonating beneath her skin. It was more.

I couldn't resist pushing. Couldn't resist tugging at the unspoken.

"Why does it bother you, *Zhyvarin*?" I asked.

Her breath hitched. But she didn't answer.

For all her control, all her intellect, she faltered. And the warmth it lit through me melted the last of my restraint.

My hands slid to her hips, easing her backward until her back met the rock wall. The pale glow of light painted shadows across her cheek, catching the edges of her features. For a moment, she still radiated tension—that stubborn refusal to surrender.

So I didn't give her the chance.

My mouth captured hers, and there was nothing gentle about it. This was possession, pure and unfiltered. A claiming I'd held back from for too long, and now, with her warm and alive in my arms, I could hold back no more. Her lips parted on a startled gasp, her hands gripping my shoulders, but she wasn't pushing me away.

I let the growl rumble deep in my chest, my wings flaring against the narrow confines before folding tightly back. Her heart beat against my ribs, insistent and wild, as I tilted my head to deepen the kiss, my tongue flicking past her lips.

Her taste wasn't just sweetness. No, it was spice and fire—a challenge that dared my control as much as it unraveled it. My claws flexed against her hips, careful not to pierce but tracing every soft curve beneath her clothes like map lines.

The kiss turned hungrier. My tail coiled around her ankle, the underside brushing bare flesh as it slid upward. She moaned into my mouth, low and throaty, sending lightning ripping through my control.

Restraint? Never heard of it.

Her fingers clutched the raised grooves of my scales. When her nails caught against the sensitive edges of my neck, I groaned. She wasn't shy. Not here. Not with me.

This was a firestorm.

"Selene," I said. My forehead rested against hers, sweat and heat mingling. My claws framed her shoulders, bracketing her wrists lightly against the wall. Gods, I didn't want her steady.

Her bottom lip caught between her teeth, swollen and glistening, and I had the urge to reclaim it, to lick and nip and taste until she dissolved entirely.

"Fuck," her voice was raw, eyes shining with something fiery and unreadable. "This is insane. We can't."

I let the smallest smile tug the edges of my mouth. "Then tell me to stop."

A laugh—breathless, intense—tumbled from her lips, and I pressed closer, our bodies aligning. Skin heated through fabric until there was no separation, and the delicious friction of her body against mine sent sparks rolling through every nerve.

"Say it," I demanded.

"Don't stop."

Her head tilted back against the stone, exposing her throat, the curve of it begging for a bite I wasn't sure she was ready for. My mouth found her jaw instead, tongue tracing the subtle line down to the hollow between her collarbones. Her breath hitched, the pulse beneath my lips pounding like drums.

"Vyne ... I—" Her words broke off into a whimper as my tail tightened, flexing with precision against the skin of her calf. The sound hit like fuel on an open flame. There was no going back now.

"Tell me to stop," I murmured against her skin, my voice ragged. "And I will."

Her response came in the form of her hands gripping the edges of my jaw and pulling me back to her lips with a fervent intensity. I devoured her, backing her tighter against the warm, uneven wall as my hands slid up, tracing along the curves of her waist and slipping under fabric until her skin sang against mine.

My talons carefully pulled at the offending

layers of clothing, easing the fabric off. Her hands gripped my shoulders tighter, pulling herself closer as the last remnants of cloth fluttered to the ground.

"Selene," her name was a plea and worship as my mouth dropped to the exposed skin at her collarbone and down to the swell of her breast. My hands explored the softness of her curves, every ridge and hollow memorized.

I didn't give her time to retreat, to think, to argue. I didn't want her doubts. I wanted her surrender. Her trust. Her everything.

Falling to my knees was an act of reverence. And I wasn't done. Not even close.

As I kissed down her stomach, her response echoed louder in the alcove.

And gods, I wanted to hear more.

The moment my lips brushed the soft heat between her thighs, her fingers twisted into my hair. Not a protest—a demand. A claiming. Her hips arched off the wall, subtle at first, then a desperate, unashamed offering, every choked-back sound vibrating through the marrow of my bones, a siren's call I couldn't resist.

Her scent was heady and salt-edged, the familiar tang of her arousal undercut by something darker, something deep that made my fangs ache. My tongue lashed upward in one long, slow, punishing swipe.

"Fuck—Vyne!" Her thighs trembled against the sides of my head, the smooth human skin in contrast with my rough scales, as I pinned her tighter to the stone. The wet slap of my tongue plunging into her, delving deep, echoed off the canyon walls, her taste, her unique essence, bursting across my senses—burnt caramel and reckless, unyielding humanity, a combination so intoxicating it threatened to shatter my control.

She tasted like war, like survival, like Volcaryth itself—fire and resilience intertwined.

Her nails scored the sensitive ridges between my shoulder blades, a painful pleasure, drawing a sound that was more beast than Drakarn. My tail, acting on its own instinct, moved up her calf with slow, sure pressure until the tip teased the soaked, sensitive apex of her thighs.

She shattered instantly.

A silent scream ripped through her, a tremor that shook her entire frame, every muscle locking as her thighs vise-gripped my skull, holding me captive. I drank her down greedily, lapping, sucking, savoring every shudder, every drop of her essence. Her scent, intensified by her release, filled the air.

"Again," I said against her quivering, exquisitely sensitive flesh, the word a rough demand, a promise, a prayer.

My tongue speared deeper, seeking out every sensitive fold, every hidden pleasure point, until she responded, a broken, beautiful sound. Her second climax came faster, harder, severe—a wounded animal sound breaking past her clenched teeth, a testament to the raw power of her pleasure.

When her knees buckled, threatening to send her collapsing, I rose in one fluid motion, pushing down my pants without ceremony. I would have ripped them to shreds with my talons if I had another pair to spare on this journey.

The scaled base of my cock glistened under the glow of the canyon, thick, dark veins pulsing with urgent need beneath the stretched, sensitive skin as the tapered tip flexed hungrily. That traitorous, wonderfully sensitive fleshy rim peeled back, revealing the flushed, engorged slit beneath—already oozing the thick, musky fluid that would brand her; a silent, invisible claim.

Her eyes darkened, pupils swallowing irises whole, leaving only pools of desire. A deep hunger mirrored my own.

"I need you," she breathed, the words a ragged plea, a challenge, an invitation.

The last thread of restraint snapped.

I hauled her legs around my hips, her soft human skin sliding against my scaled thighs, the contrast a delicious torment, my tip nudging her entrance with possessive, sure pressure. She was still spasming from her last peak, her body clenching around nothing—needy, desperate, exquisitely sensitive. The sight, the feel of her pulsing heat, nearly undid me, threatening to send me spiraling over the edge before I'd even fully claimed her.

"Watch," I commanded, my voice a low rumble, my thumb hooking her chin, forcing her gaze downward. "Watch what I do to you, *Zhyvarin*."

Her wrecked sound vibrated through every scale, every nerve ending. That flared, sensitive rim of my cock stretched her obscenely, the overstimulated nerves making her scramble for purchase against my shoulders, her fingers digging in. Inch by brutal, agonizing inch, I seated myself, pushing, stretching, filling her, until the scaled base of my shaft kissed her swollen flesh.

Her eyelids fluttered, a soft sound escaping her lips. "So ... fucking ... big—"

"You take it. All of it. You're mine, *Zhyvarin*. Made for this. Made for me."

Her answering grin was pure rebellion, a flash of the fierce, resilient spirit that had drawn me to her. She rolled her hips, taking me deeper, accepting me fully.

The world went red with untamed need.

I pistoned into her without mercy, each powerful snap of my hips slamming her into the volcanic rock. That serpentine ridge along my cock's underside stroked against her internal walls with every slow, sure withdrawal.

"Zhyvarin," I said, my breath hot against her sweat-slick throat, the word a prayer. "Mine. Mine. Always mine."

Her teeth sank into my shoulder as her climax took her. And I responded, a deep sound of release, slamming home one final, earth-shattering time. My release surged into her, claiming her from the inside out.

We hung there, suspended—her trembling legs locked around my waist, my hands embedded in the stone above her head, holding her, claiming her, possessing her. The musky, potent scent of our joining, of our mingled scents, clung to the air.

Somewhere beyond our ragged, uneven breaths, I heard Khorlar make a sound—a warning, a reminder of the world outside, of the dangers that still lurked.

Reality crashed back, unwelcome, intrusive.

But for now, none of it mattered.

My forehead pressed to hers. Selene's grip on my shoulders loosened, her fingers tracing lazy, aimless patterns across my scales, each touch a spark against my cooling skin.

I shifted, easing my weight, but not breaking the connection. Not yet. My tail unwound from her, the tip lingering to brush a slow, sure path down her spine, a silent promise. Her answering shiver was involuntary.

"You ..." she began, her voice hoarse, uneven, the word trailing off as her eyes fluttered closed.

Exhaustion finally claimed her, a heavy weight settling over her features, softening the hard edges of her spirit. Watching her sleep, vulnerable and utterly spent in my arms, something shifted. The possessive fire still burned, but it was tempered, edged with a tenderness I hadn't known I was capable of.

"You're my mate, *Zhyvarin*," I whispered.

My confession was lost to the stillness, unheard by the one person who needed to hear it. She was oblivious to the weight of the truth I'd finally acknowledged.

The irony stung. I'd spent weeks, months even, fighting this connection, fearing the consequences, the chaos it could unleash. And now, when I'd finally surrendered, when I'd finally embraced the undeniable truth ... she couldn't even hear me.

It didn't matter. We'd be home in Scalvaris soon. She'd be safe in my quarters, in my bed, soon enough. It took almost no effort for me to imagine her on my sleeping slab, hair spread out around her, the space somehow bending to her will.

Carefully, I eased us down, settling her against the curved outcropping of volcanic rock where I'd sat earlier. Her head lolled against my shoulder, her dark hair spilling across my chest. She murmured something unintelligible, a soft, sleepy sound that tugged at something deep within.

I wrapped my arms around her in a protective embrace, my wings shielding her from any threat. I would protect her. I would fight for her. I would do whatever it took to keep her safe, to keep her by my side.

She was my mate.

And I wasn't letting her go.

TWENTY-TWO
SELENE

Everything on Volcaryth was designed to kill. Knowing that didn't make breathing any easier.

Worse was the rhythm around me. Vyne's wing-beats. Steady. Unyielding. With every stroke, the pressure of his body shifted. I was cradled against his chest, his scaled arms locked around me. My brain told me I was safe. My stupid human, survival-instinct brain disagreed.

And I was trying—desperately—to survive my own mind.

His warmth clung to me. I swore I could still smell him on me. And my body ached in all the places that reminded me just what we'd done together. Vyne was life and danger wrapped in one unbearable pull, and after last night ...

Fuck.

The memory of his lips, his touch—of the way we'd fit together—made my heart kick against my ribs. Sparks of what we'd shared still crackled where the tips of his claws brushed my side. I wanted nothing more than to lie back down with him and stay lost in the pleasure.

But then the weight returned: what I *should* have been doing. The vyrathis. The healers. The hollow-eyed, rasping bodies in the healing caverns. I'd lost hours with Vyne. Hours we could have been flying back. And now, with the precious container of vyrathis tucked in my pack, every second screamed at me. Time we didn't have.

It didn't matter that both Vyne and Khorlar had made it clear we couldn't fly at night, that they needed to rest their wings.

We could rest when the healers weren't dying.

The thought made my chest tighten, and I shifted. His arms locked firmer, claws coiling protectively under the curve of my back. "Don't wriggle," he growled, voice low against the wind. "Unless you want to test how good I am at catching humans mid-fall."

I kept my tone dry. "I wasn't planning on taking any dives. How much farther?"

Vyne's eyes narrowed. "Not long," he said. "We'll be able to enter through one of the sky shafts from this approach. No need to climb through the tunnels."

Ahead, Khorlar flew steadily, massive gray wings militaristic in their precision. They didn't falter, even with the human shape clinging weakly to his broad chest.

Reika.

From my position, she looked impossibly small, a curled shadow cradled against Khorlar's scaled arms. The pale streak of her skin was faint against the muted gray of his leathers. But even from a distance, I could see the shaking. Her wrists trembled, and her head slumped awkwardly. Exhaustion had her in a chokehold, and the rough lines of fever were unmistakable.

I should have done something for it before we left. The red streaks webbed around the cuts on her arms and shoulders—delicate but dangerous threads that coiled inward. Infection. Her breathing, too shallow, too labored, told me enough.

It wasn't the sickness plaguing the healers. This was simpler, caused by exhaustion and dirt. But it could be just as deadly.

One crisis at a time, Selene. Deal with the healers first.

A shift in the air cut through my thoughts. The wind grew sharper, warmer, as we descended through the narrow sky shaft that would take us into Scalvaris.

Vyne angled his wings, leaning into the wind as he adjusted our trajectory. My stomach flipped as the updrafts pushed against us. Every muscle in Vyne's body tensed as we veered closer.

"It's safe?" The edge in my voice was unavoidable.

Vyne's lips twitched. "I'd hardly take you down here if it wasn't."

I hated that I liked the quiet authority in his voice.

Khorlar shifted positions, descending faster, his broad gray wings slicing through the heat. He landed heavily just ahead of us, raised claws creating a protective barrier as Reika shifted weakly.

A sick, horrible sound rasped from her throat.

The second I was on solid ground, I rushed to Khorlar.

"Get her straight to the healing caverns," I snapped. Duty cleared my mind. "She's burning up."

Khorlar's gaze was steady. He said nothing, simply turning toward the nearest corridor and carrying her away.

Vyne touched my arm. "Selene, I—"

"No," I couldn't do this now, whatever it was. "The vyrathis first." Vyne and I ... there was something there. Something real. I wanted it so bad it hurt. But I could deal with the delay. Delaying our mission meant death for the healers.

Emotions had to come later.

The passageways narrowed, the unbroken stone brushing against my arms as I ducked low into the heat of the city. But my pace didn't falter, even as the familiar glow of heat crystals guided me. My mind stayed locked on the bodies waiting below.

Waiting. Fighting. Clinging to the edge of existence.

I couldn't fail them.

When we reached the healing caverns, it felt like death. The thick, acrid scent of sickness pooled, mingling with the tang of sweaty bodies and burnt herbs. It was worse than I remembered.

Rachel and Kaiya were in the center, heads bent over one of the makeshift tables overflowing with vials and crushed plant matter. Smudged lines of exhaustion painted Rachel's features, dark shadows pooling beneath her eyes.

Kaiya's hands flew between a mortar and pestle, crushing something with frantic energy, her curls plastered damp and flat against her temples. They were both close to collapsing—two women, stretched far beyond their limits, but still fighting.

A choked cough from a nearby bed drew my

focus. One of the healers—a broad-shouldered Drakarn male—shook violently, his once-brilliant red scales dull and marred with dark, web-like veins. His breathing was shallow, punctuated by strained, wet gasps.

I looked to the other beds. The sight sent a sharp twist deep into my chest. The healers were crumbling. The same spread of bruises marred every weak body. Wings hung limp. Mysha's bed was at the far end, her breathing low and weak, but, thank god, steady. She still had a chance.

"Selene!" Rachel's voice cut through the haze. Her relief was visible. "Tell me you have it."

I swung the pack off my back, setting it on the table with a thud that made Kaiya jump, though her hands kept working. "Yes. Here."

Rachel's hands were on it instantly, pulling the container free with care, her fingers quick. For all her exhaustion, she moved with practiced precision.

"How much did you find?" Rachel asked. Her words were coated in cautious hope.

"I hope it's enough."

Rachel nodded in sharp agreement, already moving to prepare the medicine. Another cough dragged my attention to the far side of the cavern, where a younger healer thrashed weakly.

My gut clenched.

Behind me, Vyne cleared his throat. Of course, always watching, always steady, always too near and too far. His presence loomed, an anchor I couldn't let drag me down. Not now.

"You need rest, *Zhyvarin*," Vyne said quietly. "Let's go to our quarters."

Our quarters?

What?

His words landed, and my brain stuttered. I snapped my gaze to him. "Our quarters?" My voice came out ragged. "What are you talking about?"

We'd slept together twice. Since when did that mean living together? Or was I jumping to conclusions? A week on the surface of Volcaryth had nearly knocked me out, and relief now was mixed with exhaustion. Whatever Vyne was saying, I was probably misunderstanding. We were just ... hell, I didn't know.

You know it's more than that.

I shoved the thought away.

His wings shifted. He spoke low but steady, each syllable careful. "You need rest. You've done enough. More than enough. Come home with me."

A bitter laugh clawed up my throat. "Enough? You honestly think this is enough?" My hands jerked up, motioning toward the rows of beds. Drakarn lay on them, motionless or writhing, their breaths rasping. "In case you haven't noticed, they're still dying, Vyne. Until that stops, nothing is enough."

The truth scraped my throat, but I didn't care.

Tension rippled through him, though his voice remained calm. Too calm. "I'm not telling you to stop," he replied slowly. Measured. "But even you know you can't pour from an empty vessel. You need rest. You need time to—"

"To what?" Anger flared, hot and sharp. "Rest? Recuperate? Learn to live with failure while I sit back and watch them die?" The words tumbled out, and I couldn't pull them back.

His gaze dropped, briefly, to my hands. The tremble betrayed me. I curled my fingers into fists.

"You're my mate," he said, softer now, but the word shook me to my core. "I won't let you burn yourself out."

Mate. Mate. Mate. It seemed to echo off the walls around us.

"Stop." The word came fast, sharp, exploding from somewhere deep in me. My voice cracked. I didn't mean it to come out that way—cold and rough —but it was the only thing I had. A shield. "Just stop. Please."

The tension between us shifted. He stilled, expression hardening, his wings pulling close to his body. His eyes—so sharp, so unrelenting—found mine again. He didn't falter.

"You're mine." It was a declaration.

Those words—those two damn words—crushed me.

Shock surged up, tangling with everything else I'd shoved down—fear, exhaustion, anger, grief. How could he say that? How could he just ... drop this on me *now*, here, surrounded by dying healers? How could he say *mine* as though it wasn't going to rip me open?

"I—"

There was too much. Too much to feel, too much to think, and no space for anything in the middle of this crisis. My chest tightened, and I tore my gaze from his, desperate to focus on anything else.

This didn't make sense.

But my body knew otherwise. Even as fear and doubt trembled through my limbs, I felt a steady beating in my chest. Something undeniable. And I hated it. I hated how it pulled.

"I can't do this," I bit out. My hands clenched, nails digging crescents into my palms. "Not now. I can't—"

Vyne stepped closer, his movements careful, as if I was something fragile. "You're overwhelmed," he said low, a hint of a growl threading his voice. "But I'm not wrong. I know you feel it."

I shook my head, hard. I needed to stop this, stop him. "Don't call me that—your mate. I can't—"

"You *are*." His tone unraveled me further. "You've been mine from the moment I first saw you. This," he gestured between us, "is too strong to ignore. I've tried."

Every muscle tensed. Fight or flight screamed in tandem, and yet, I couldn't do either.

Because he wasn't backing down. He wasn't walking away. And that terrified me more than anything.

But there was no room for this. Not now. Not here. Not when my responsibilities threatened to crush me.

Someone cleared their throat. Kaiya was standing a few paces behind us. Her face was pale, her shoulders tight. "Sorry to interrupt," she said tightly, her eyes briefly flicking between me and Vyne. "Selene, I need your help. Rachel needs a second set of hands preparing the vyrathis extract so we can start administering it ASAP."

She didn't have to say more.

"Of course," I replied, stepping toward her. My priorities were crystal clear. I shot Vyne a glance over my shoulder. "Go," I told him. "I ... We'll ..."

I had no idea what I was supposed to say.

Vyne tensed, but he didn't argue. And with one last lingering look that burned, he turned and left.

Kaiya seemed to shrink in on herself. "Thank god you're here," she muttered, already rushing back toward the central table.

I threw myself into the work. It was that or think of Vyne. And if I did that, I might actually go crazy.

Night had settled over the makeshift infirmary, but no rest came with it—only a thick, stifling heaviness that pressed in, as though the stone around us devoured every flicker of hope. That same oppressive feeling slithered beneath my scales and knotted in my chest.

I carefully removed a half-formed metal clamp from the forge, its heated grip making my claws tingle. This was the fifth clamp I'd made in the last hour. They were simple and a little crude, but maybe they'd save lives.

Usually I'd craft weapons there—blades to fight things with teeth and claws. Now, I was shaping medical tools that Selene and the healers needed to survive.

Once the clamp had cooled in a bucket of water,

I slung it with a few others in the crook of my arm and set off down the corridor. Darkness pressed close in these tunnels, broken only by the sullen glow of heat crystals embedded in the rock. My steps fell into a determined rhythm, matching the tension in my thoughts.

I'd already cursed myself a hundred times for how I'd handled our arrival back to Scalvaris. This wasn't much, but I would give her what help I could, show her that I knew just how important she was. To the city.

And to me.

When I entered the infirmary, it was the usual sight of cramped beds and tired faces, human and Drakarn alike. The air felt thicker than the forge's blaze—clogged with infection, antiseptics, exhaustion. A few Drakarn, sporting half-mended scales, dozed or stared off in silence. Human healers bustled quietly, measuring powders, boiling water, checking pulses.

Selene stood across the room, tending to a bronze-scaled Drakarn who looked dangerously fragile. She leaned in, gently pressing a cloth to a reopened wound at his neck. There was a careful tenderness in her movements, but I saw how stiffly she held herself.

I ached to cross the room, to help. To pick her up

and *make* her rest. But I held back. She glanced up, looked at me, and then away as if I wasn't there at all.

Kaiya beckoned me over to a table crowded with half-empty bowls, jars, and fresh bandages. The pungent smell of herbs stung my nostrils. She clutched a mortar and pestle, her eyes dark with fatigue. When I placed the clamps on the table, she gave me a weary smile.

"How many more can you make?" she asked.

"As many as you need."

She nodded. "We'll need plenty. Anything you've got, really."

I only nodded. My gaze slid to where Selene was gathering supplies near a cracked crate. Her hair was falling out of the string she'd used to tie it back. Even from there, I saw fresh shadows under her eyes. She rose and walked toward us with purpose, looking at me once, so briefly I might have imagined it.

"Are those the new clamps?" she asked Kaiya. I might as well have not existed.

Kaiya gestured at the metal pieces. "Yes—Vyne just brought them."

Selene lifted one of the clamps, working the hinge with her fingers. For a second, I thought I saw approval in her eyes. Then her expression went flat. "They'll do." She set the clamp back onto the table and marched off. My chest tightened at the dismissal.

This was worse than I thought.

A fit of coughing erupted nearby, sharp and grating. One of the sick—an older male I recognized but couldn't name—lurched in his bed.

Selene was already moving. "Kaiya, get me a clamp—and more bandages, quickly!" She rushed over, fear barely masked behind focus.

I was right on her heels, crossing the space in a single stride. "I've got him," I said, bracing the convulsing Drakarn's upper body. His tail flailed dangerously near Selene, and I tightened my grip, trying to keep her out of harm's way. My own tail shot out, wrapping with his and wrangling it down like we were wrestling.

The smell of blood tainted the air; the Drakarn's wound spurted a fresh stream of foul fluid. Selene pressed her hand to his cheek. "Easy," she soothed, though I could see the fear in her eyes. "You're tearing your wound wider. Let us help you."

He roared again, but his voice cracked, the delirium looking painfully close to panic. Claws raked the air, nearly catching my arm. I shifted, tucking one arm under his and gripping tight so Selene could work.

Kaiya dashed back with bandages. Selene

snatched them, her face set in fierce concentration. She juggled disinfectant and the clamp, pressing the wound's edges together while the Drakarn bucked. My arms trembled with the force of holding him.

"Stay still," I growled into his ear. He gave another ragged bellow, head snapping back against my shoulder.

Selene finally fitted the clamp into place, securing the torn flesh. The male let out a guttural groan, his body dropping from fevered tension to exhausted stillness. "Almost done," she whispered, grabbing a suture kit and stitching around the clamp's edges. Her touch was deft, every movement swift but precise. When she finished, she exhaled, pressing one hand over his wound to keep the clamp from slipping.

I let out a long breath, easing my hold. The Drakarn sagged onto the cot with a weak moan. Blood matted my forearm—mine or his, I didn't know. My shoulder stung from the line of fresh cuts, but I barely noticed it. I was too busy watching Selene.

Her eyes lifted to meet mine. For an instant, we were the only two people in the room. "Thank you," she said.

A ripple of something like longing passed between us. The moment cracked, and she pulled away, dabbing blood from her hands as she spoke to Kaiya. Without another word, she slipped into the corridor to wash. My entire body hummed with tension. I wanted to follow her, demand she let me hold her, comfort her, take her away from this place. But the braced line of her shoulders was a warning: not now.

Kaiya gave me a quick nod before turning back to the patient. The healing caverns settled down as the crisis ebbed, leaving me with nothing to do but stare at the space where Selene had disappeared.

Anger churned in me that I couldn't fix this, that I couldn't protect her from any more pain. She needed room to breathe. All I wanted was to shield her from the world so she could.

The glow of crystals lit my path back to the small, stuffy forge. A half-finished anvil sat waiting, flickers of heat dancing over the coals. I moved toward it, hammer in hand. Work was the one thing I could do without question, the one way I could still stand beside Selene—indirectly if not literally.

Drawing a deep breath, I plunged a fresh bar of steel into the embers, coaxing the orange glow until the metal softened. I withdrew it with a pair of tongs and laid it on the anvil. Sparks flew at my first strike, bright motes that collapsed before hitting the ground. My muscles ached from overuse, sweat already slicking my scales. But I kept swinging, forging a tool this time—a delicate, curved retractor that Selene and Kaiya might use to hold tissue in place for sutures. If I could improve even one procedure, maybe Selene would suffer fewer nightmares of watching her patients bleed out.

Each blow of the hammer became a vow: I would do everything in my power to prove I was more than trouble and hunger. I'd stand beside her, bolster her when she wavered. If the best I could do was to twist steel into useful shapes, then I'd do it until my arms failed. In this hush, I made a promise to her, to us, even if she didn't hear it right now.

If she needed space, I'd give it. If she needed time, I'd wait. But I would not vanish.

I placed another steel bar into the coals. I wasn't stopping until dawn. That was the one thing that felt certain: keep forging, keep giving, keep proving. No matter how many blows it took.

TWENTY-FOUR
SELENE

I paced through the makeshift infirmary, boots scraping softly across uneven stone. Somewhere in my mind, Vyne's voice kept replaying like an echo stuck on repeat.

"You're mine."

I tried to pretend I had everything under control, but that declaration rattled inside me, refusing to fade.

The Drakarn's ragged breathing pulled my attention back to the present. Their condition was improving, but each breath still sounded like it fought through a layer of sickness that didn't fully want to let go. The vyrathis extract had helped stabilize them—enough that their labored wheezing wasn't quite so ominous—but it wasn't a miracle. We had to wait for healing to happen naturally.

I hated leaning on hope that felt so fragile.

I stopped by Mysha's cot, checking her temperature with the back of my hand. The soft glimmer of her scales was reassuring. She felt hot, but not feverish. Her chest rose and fell in a steadier rhythm than yesterday, but there was still a long way to go.

I exhaled slowly, letting my hand drop back to my side. The memory of Vyne heated my thoughts. His gaze, his strong grip. I was trying to push those feelings aside, but each time I remembered the slow burn in his eyes, my stomach fluttered traitorously.

Now was *not* the time for that. These people needed me focused. I shook my head, forcing my mind to return to the scene in front of me.

Then there was Reika

She looked so small in a space intended for towering Drakarn warriors. Her breathing was shallow but steady, and her forehead glistened with fresh sweat. At least the fever was no longer raging like it had been. She didn't stir when I approached.

But I wasn't her only visitor.

Khorlar watched her with a stillness that made my skin prickle. I swallowed, unsure if I should say anything. The hush in the cavern was almost loud in a strange way, and I didn't want to disturb it.

Khorlar rose in one swift motion, ignoring me

outright, and marched away, tall frame melting into the shadows near the exit.

What was he even doing there in the first place?

I kneaded my temple with my thumb before lowering myself at Reika's side. Gingerly, I brushed a damp lock of hair off her forehead. Her breathing hitched under my touch, though she didn't wake. Dull purple bruises mottled her arms. I hated to think of what had been done to her.

The hush abruptly broke as distant footsteps raced toward us. The way they thudded—a rapid, uneven cadence—made the fine hairs on my neck rise. Kira lurched into the healing cavern, looking winded and wild-eyed.

I stood and took a step toward her, worry punching through my own exhaustion. "Is everything okay?"

Her gaze darted from bed to bed. She didn't respond to me; I'm not even sure she saw me.

"Where is she?" Kira's voice rang through the cavern, cutting through the moan of the sick and stirring an uneasy flutter among the Drakarn who weren't fully unconscious. "Where's Larissa?"

Her eyes were frantic. "Kira," I edged closer, "who are you looking for?" But I had a sick feeling in my stomach. I already knew.

Kira's chest heaved, words tumbling out almost incoherently. "My sister. They said there was another human. That you found someone. Where—"

Then she spotted Reika. The color drained from Kira's face as she hurried over, dropping to her knees with a raw cry. My pulse stuttered. I'd never seen someone's heart break right in front of me before.

"No," she gasped, voice dissolving in a half-sob, half-denial. "No, no, no—"

She gripped Reika's arms, as though if she held on tightly enough, Reika might become the sister she was so desperately wishing for. Her one wrenching sob tore at my gut. I stepped in behind Kira and crouched down.

"I'm sorry." It felt so hollow.

Tears rolled unchecked down her face. "I thought if I just kept hoping ..." Her voice broke, and she bowed her head until her forehead touched the edge of the cot. "She's dead, isn't she? They're all dead."

My own heart twisted. "We can't know that," I said, as gentle as I could manage. "But maybe Reika can tell us what she knows. When she wakes up."

There was no telling if Reika had been on the same ship we'd been on. It made sense. How many ways were there for humans to end up on Volcaryth? But jumping to conclusion could give Kira false hope. And she was already on the edge of falling apart.

She sniffed, nodding in a jerky motion, tears still brimming in her eyes. Slowly, she loosened her hold on Reika. Just as she was getting herself steady, a new presence disrupted the quiet.

Vega entered in her usual brash fashion, scanning the rows of beds with a quick, sweeping look. "So we found another human. The guys in charge are going to *love* that."

I was already bracing myself. "Not now, Vega."

She raised an eyebrow, glancing at me and then at Kira's hunched form. "Don't get your hackles up. Am I the only one that remembers that we're here on sufferance? Or did you forget how they almost killed Orla for a bit of accidental trespassing? As far as they're concerned, more humans equal more trouble. I'm trying to keep us alive here."

Kira rose unsteadily, turning on Vega. "If you're so eager for doom and gloom, go preach it somewhere else," she snapped. "We don't need you making everyone feel worse."

Vega's eyes flicked over her. She looked as though she might lob a retort but then seemed to think better of it. An uneasy shrug took over her stance. "Fine. But this place is a powder keg waiting for a spark."

I pinched the bridge of my nose, a headache nudging its way behind my eyes. "Let's just not," I said, keeping my tone level through sheer force of will. "We can't afford it." I hesitated, then exhaled. "Why are you even here, Vega?"

"I'm a helper, didn't you know? I've been in here every day, cleaning up unspeakable messes and trying to keep the dragon-monsters alive." Her face wrinkled in distaste.

"Let's not call our patients monsters." I dreaded to consider her bedside manner.

Vega shrugged and walked off to get started with her shift. I didn't try to stop her. She had an attitude, but we needed the hands.

The silence she left behind felt loaded, all the more claustrophobic in the dim light. Kira gave me a look so full of exhaustion that I felt another wave of guilt rising.

Kira brushed her knuckles across her damp cheeks. Anger and sorrow mingled in her eyes. "Let me know if she says anything about Larissa."

I nodded. "I promise."

Without another word, she spun on her heel and headed for the exit. My heart ached for her—and for all of us, really. We were trapped beneath this mountain, clinging to uncertain alliances and half-fixes.

I looked at Reika. She was still, aside from the

movement of her breathing. Then my own doubts started circling—and inevitably, my thoughts landed on Vyne. I told myself I was just tired, but even the mention of his name in my head made something hot twist in my gut.

I stood there, fists clenched, letting the memory of *"You're mine"* pound against the inside of my skull.

He had the shittiest timing on Earth. Or, well, Volcaryth.

What would happen if I gave in? If I let myself believe? My stomach knotted, torn between wanting him in some undeniable way and knowing I shouldn't risk it—not now, with so much chaos.

I owed Orla an apology. Looking back, my advice to her about her situation with her own Drakarn warrior felt glib. I'd even joked about wanting one of my own.

I had no idea what that meant.

"Are we going to talk about it?" I nearly jumped out of my seat when Kaiya's question lashed me like a whip.

"The healers are doing better. We can figure out Reika's situation once she's up." There was so much to do and not enough hands, but we were making do. "Is Rachel sleeping?"

"I hope so, but come on, Selene." She sat down

on a stool beside me and gave me a *look*. "You slept here last night. Are you hiding from Mr. Tall, Green, and Obsessed with you?"

Yes.

No.

I didn't know.

I groaned. "Can we not? Please."

"Are you one of those people who solves everyone else's problems while letting your own fester?" she asked, diagnosing me faster than any therapist back on Earth.

"I'm one of those people who doesn't let others die because I have issues in my personal life." It felt like a weak retort, but I didn't have anything else.

Kaiya stared at me, waiting for me to break.

I wouldn't. I was stronger than that. I didn't need to vent. I could handle this on my own.

Who was I kidding?

"We barely know each other. The mission was all stress and excitement and ... fuck if I know. And now he's telling me I'm his mate, as if I have time to deal with that while all of *this* is happening." I spread my hand out, gesturing towards the healing Drakarn. "What was he thinking?"

"Oh, no, you're totally right on that part. His timing sucks. But I saw the way he looked at you. He wasn't lying."

"I know that!" I clamped my mouth shut, like that might call back the words.

If I knew all that, why was I stressing?

I groaned. "Do you have any advice, or are you just going to ask pointed questions?"

"You don't need advice, just a little kick in the ass. Our lives are completely messed up. It's not like any of this was planned. So maybe embrace the good stuff?"

Before I could say more, she patted me on the shoulder and walked away to tend to one of the moaning healers.

I didn't want to obsess over Vyne. I didn't want to think about what it meant if I was his mate.

The problem was, I couldn't stop.

With a grunt, I got up and walked away from Reika and resumed checking the other beds. Mysha stirred under my hand, blinking in brief confusion before drifting back into sleep. I listened for any trace of that deep, hacking rasp that had haunted them all before, but it seemed to be fading. Hope flickered inside me, fragile but alive.

After finishing my rounds, I tipped my head from side to side, stretching until my spine popped. The oppressive space pressed in. It smelled like damp stone and stale air, and the walls felt closer than they had hours ago. I needed to leave this ward, if only for a few minutes.

But as I leaned against the wall, the rasping coughs of the healers echoed in my ears, and under that were Vyne's unforgettable words.

You're mine.

TWENTY-FIVE
VYNE

The forge roared and glowed. Familiar heat pressed against my lungs, each breath thick and laced with iron tang. The hammer in my hand rose and fell in a vicious rhythm, a metallic heartbeat echoing through the stone. Each strike against the battered blade on the anvil should have eased the discord growing inside me.

It didn't.

My arms burned from fatigue, sweat coursing over my scales, but I couldn't stop. Every swing was a question I couldn't answer, a frustration I couldn't name. If I kept hammering, maybe I could outrun the regret that gnawed at the corners of my mind:

Selene.

She was everything I'd never asked for—fury, a spark, and a fragile softness all tangled in one. The memory of her lived in every breath, every flare of muscle. A storm I couldn't calm and didn't want to. But that storm had pulled away, and the fear of losing her forever lodged deep in me, more suffocating than the forge's heat.

It was all my own damned fault. Some need had possessed me to claim her then and there, as if exhaustion hadn't weighed heavy on us, as if Selene hadn't spent the last several days, all edges frayed with worry for the healers.

I drove the hammer down harder, as though I could pound answers from the metal. Sparks ricocheted in orange bursts, scattering into the air. The steel warped beneath each blow, but no matter how many times I struck, the chaos in me only grew.

A heavy presence filled the doorway behind me before he spoke. I knew who it was by the slow scrape of his talons against stone, by the weight in the air that always announced him. Khorlar.

"You'll ruin the blade," he observed, his deep voice steady. "Or yourself."

I scowled, not taking my eyes off the battered metal. "I can fix it."

"Can you?"

Clenching my jaw, I lifted the hammer again. The strike was so forceful it jarred my shoulder. A rough growl tore from my chest. "Why are you here?"

Khorlar folded his massive arms across his dark-gray scales. "Because I'd rather not see you destroy good steel."

I barked a short laugh. "Close your eyes, then."

Silence thickened, punctuated only by the clang of metal. My wings twitched, restless, but I forced myself to keep going. I couldn't stop, or I'd feel too much.

"Is this about the human?" Khorlar asked, finally.

My grip tightened around the hammer, claws scraping against the worn handle. "She has a name."

He inclined his head, unruffled by my sharp tone. "Selene," he corrected. "Another human mate?"

I slammed the hammer down, and the blade cracked under the impact. I tossed the hammer and the ruined blade aside.

"You don't know a damned thing about it."

He let out a low snort. "I haven't suggested that I do."

Fury flared, but I caught myself. This wasn't just anger—it was fear, an old enemy wearing a new face. "She made her desires, or lack thereof, very clear."

"Do you think that sound doesn't carry in a

canyon? Because what I heard wasn't a lack of desire."

He was lucky I'd dropped the hammer. Rage flared hot and fast. He had *no right* to hear what sounds my mate made when I gave her pleasure, no right to intrude or say a word about it.

My heart thumped in a ragged rhythm, answering a call deeper than logic. Selene was mine —even if she doubted it.

"Leave me." I didn't need his prying or his opinion. Khorlar had no love for the humans, and if he spoke one sour word about my mate, I'd be forced to test the ruined blade sitting in the discard pile.

He hesitated for a moment before doing as I asked.

I closed my eyes and swallowed hard. I was hitting the wrong target. No amount of metal would shape itself into glass. Thunder rumbled in me, a pulse of longing that tasted like desperation.

Sweat dripped from my brow, the forge's heat melding with the searing temperature of my own blood. My temples pounded, but this time, I let the ache in, forced myself to feel it. If I was going to fight for Selene, I needed every ounce of pain, every shred of need. This bond was stupid, maddening, and the only thing that felt real.

My heart lurched as her scent tickled my nose. I

thought it was a phantom at first, but she stood in the doorway, haloed by the forge's angry glow.

She looked exhausted—hair tousled, worry lines carved into her brow—but her gaze was steady on mine. She smelled like the healing caverns: herbs, sweat, and under it all was just *her*. Something I wanted to drown in.

Selene and I stood there, the forge sputtering sparks that died in the hush between us. When she finally spoke, her voice had the rough scrape of resolve and heartbreak. "I think we should talk."

I forced a breath, setting my shoulders. "All right," I managed.

Everything in me wanted to yank her close and demand she believe that she was mine, that I'd keep her safe. But I held back. I had to.

It was hell.

Her arms were wrapped around herself like a shield. The light highlighted the tired circles beneath her eyes. I hated knowing I was part of why they were there.

"Yesterday ...," she said softly, "Vyne, I—" she huffed out a breath. "We've known each other for a week, and you tried to take over my life like you owned it."

My immediate instinct was to argue. I dug my fangs into my tongue until I tasted copper. I wouldn't mess this up again. Not now. Not with her.

She swallowed hard. "My entire life flipped on its head the second I ended up here. And every time I think I'm adjusting, something else breaks under my feet. Everyone freaked the fuck out with Orla and Rath. And don't think I haven't heard what people whisper about Darrokar and Terra. You and I, it's ..."

"It's real." I wasn't going to push, but I couldn't let this go. "I told myself to stay away. I tried. Gods below, I tried." I took half a step forward and forced myself to stop. "Do you think I want to bring trouble to you?"

I could almost taste the fear behind her anger, the vulnerability she tried so hard to hide. My claws twitched, itching to grab her and prove how real it was. But I'd come too close before, only to see her shut down from the weight of it.

I stepped forward until only a breath separated us. Softly, I cupped her chin, forcing her gaze up to mine. "I'm your mate, *Zhyvarin*," I said, letting every thread of truth coil in my voice. "It means someone in this gods-forsaken world will fight for you, bleed for you ... die for you, if that's what it takes."

Her lip quivered, and for a moment, I was sure she'd bolt. But she stayed.

"The others need me," she whispered, as if it were an apology. "I can't allow myself to be distracted, not when people are dying, when—"

"Selene," her name was a vow. "I don't want to strip you of your responsibilities. I just want to stand beside you while you fulfill them. Let me."

Emotions flickered over her face: anger, hope ... terror. One by one, they warred for dominance. Finally, she dropped her head, breath shuddering. "I'm not sure how," she murmured. "And now, you're telling me to open up ... That you want me as what, exactly?"

"Everything," I breathed. "I want everything."

Before I could stop myself, I dropped to my knees, the motion swift and sure, every last shred of control leaving me as I knelt in front of her. My hands moved to frame her hips, steady but reverent, claws curling under against the soft fabric of her clothes without piercing—without risking breaking her.

She deserved better than my fire. But I couldn't stop offering it to her.

"What will it take to make you mine?"

Her eyes widened. But she didn't run. With a single exhale, it seemed like she let go of something heavy. "I think ..." Her words came quietly, voice hitching. "I think I've been yours for a while now, whether I liked it or not."

The heat in my chest flared brighter, roaring hot and unrelenting as though she'd poured molten steel into my ribs. Her confession settled deep in the raw places I'd been trying desperately to keep from fracturing further. It wasn't an admission; it was a collision—a force slamming into me with the weight of all the words she hadn't said before.

For the first time in weeks, the fire inside me didn't feel like it was trying to hollow me out. It felt like fuel.

"Then stay," I said softly, my voice hoarse but unwavering. The words cut low from the depths of my chest, layers of feeling I'd long buried spilling freely now. "Stay with me."

Her lips trembled, a breathless exhale escaping before she dropped to her knees, her hands finally reaching for me. And gods help me, the way she touched me—light but certain, like she was still deciding if she should've claimed me sooner—ignited the only answer I had left.

Mine.

Always mine.

The forge roared hotter around us, and I embraced the burn.

TWENTY-SIX
SELENE

It was hard to tell if the room itself was hot or if Vyne was the one heating it. Probably both.

His room was buried deep in Scalvaris—some hybrid of a forge, a bedroom, and an artist's den. Not far from where I stood, a broad stone slab topped with silks served as a bed. If I looked too long at it, my heart started hammering.

But Vyne was the main attraction.

He was standing near the center of the room, wings half-furled, glancing my way with this tension that made me think of coiled springs. His scales caught the light, shimmering in that dark-green shade that reminded me of polished emeralds. Though he wasn't moving, he was brimming with energy—a wildfire held behind a flimsy barrier.

He didn't say a word. Didn't have to. I knew

exactly what he was waiting for, and I realized I'd been waiting just as desperately. My feet closed the distance between us, while inside me, everything seemed to stutter and surge at once.

He met me halfway, wings curving around in a slow sweep that made my breath catch. It was intimate—those tough, scaled membranes forming a secluded world for just the two of us. One of his hands rose, thumb brushing my jaw. A quick spark lit my nerve endings, and my focus tunneled in on him alone.

I wanted to say something—anything—but my mind was too tangled by the intensity in his gaze. His breath fanned across my cheek, warm as the forge's embers, and my lips parted in anticipation before he moved. Then he was there, leaning in, claiming my mouth in a single, searing kiss that stole the last of my composure.

That first contact struck like lightning—pure, charged need. My eyes fluttered shut as tingles raced from the press of his lips to the tips of my fingers. I clung to his shoulders, half afraid my legs might give out from the sheer heat of him. Each slide of his mouth over mine stoked that inner flame, making my pulse pound so loudly that nothing else existed. The worries, the obligations ... they dissolved into the background noise of the world.

His tongue teased the seam of my lips, a coaxing pressure that sent a small gasp tumbling out. He seized the sound, deepening the kiss even more. When his fangs grazed my lower lip, drawing a startled, breathless hitch from my chest, a surge of hunger jolted through me. His taste was salt and fire, a sensation that set every nerve alight.

I melted into him, fingers digging into the hard muscle of his back as though anchoring myself to reality. But reality shifted—narrowing down to the rough planes of his body beneath my hands and the muted growl resonating behind our joined mouths. Instinct took over, guiding me to open for him farther. His kiss grew more urgent and confident, each slow, thorough stroke enough to make me forget breathing.

The world tilted as he guided me backward, the edges of my vision hazy with want. My spine met the platform behind me in a less than gentle thump, jolting us just enough to break our lips apart. A ragged breath left me, matching his own uneven exhale. Our eyes met in that heartbeat of distance, and then he tugged me close again, our mouths catching in another all-consuming kiss that left no air between us.

I didn't give him time to ask if I was sure—my answer was obvious. I grabbed a handful of his top, tugging him closer. He made a low, rough sound. Next thing I knew, he was slicing my shirt off with the edge of a claw, neat as a seam ripper. A startled laugh escaped me, cut short when his lips covered mine again.

He tasted urgent, like we'd put this off for far too long, even if it had only been a day. His wings shifted, brushing my bare shoulders. Everything felt fevered. When his tongue slid down my throat, I couldn't stop the shudder, or the way my fingers fisted in his hair, searching for something to hold onto.

He had me up on the stone bed before I realized it, his body wedging between my knees. My thighs squeezed around him, and for a wild second, I remembered how strong he was—this Drakarn warrior who could bend steel and slice rock. Somehow, all that power was cradling me with a careful sweetness.

And he was all mine.

His kisses skimmed my collarbone, teeth grazing in a way that made me arch into him. Electricity fizzed along my nerves. I reached for the fastenings of his leathers, fumbling them loose, while he slid his hand down my side, claws pricking gently in warning. That tiny sting had my pulse kicking even faster.

Once his chest straps dropped away, I paused to

stare. The crystals in the room cast him in half-shadows, revealing lines of muscle and scale, plus faint silver scars from old battles. I'd never get used to how gorgeous he was in his brutal, inhuman way.

Now I had all the time in the world to stare. No Ignarath warriors were chasing us down. The healers had the vyrathis they needed to heal.

And Vyne was my mate.

I was still getting used to that.

Vyne shifted closer, pressing me into the welcoming softness of the silks. He trailed kisses over my stomach, hungry but unhurried. I gasped when he finally moved between my thighs. His breath sent tingles through my hypersensitive skin.

Then that tongue of his, longer and rougher than any human's, flicked against me. He traced the length of my slit, flicking and teasing in a way that sent electric jolts through me. Each pass of that rough tongue felt shockingly vivid, as if he had tapped directly into my nerve endings. He lapped at me like he was savoring the finest honey, slow and sensuous.

I trembled beneath him, skin flushed and hypersensitive. When he found my clit and zeroed in on it, I nearly screamed. He circled the sensitive nub with the tip of his tongue, just barely grazing it, until I was shuddering and writhing helplessly against the slab.

His wings enveloped us like a cocoon of heat and anticipation.

Just as he had my climax coiled tight, ready to spring, he abruptly withdrew. I made a strangled noise of protest, hips bucking uselessly. Vyne chuckled low and sultry, the sound reverberating through me.

"You want more, *Zhyvarin?*" he purred, eyes glinting wickedly in the firelight.

I could only moan in response, utterly at his mercy. The knowledge only seemed to fuel his desire.

I tried to stifle a cry. No chance. It tore out anyway, echoing off the stone walls. He made a satisfied sound deep in his chest, the vibration nearly pushing me over the edge. My fingers clamped around his shoulders, nails scraping at his scales. Each pass of that wicked tongue felt shockingly vivid, until I was right at the point of toppling into oblivion.

But he pulled back before I finished. My outraged whimper must've amused him, because he had a half-smile on his lips when he crawled back up my body. That look disappeared into another kiss, scorching and immediate. I could feel the press of his cock—heavy and alien, with that odd, flared lip at the tip—stretching me in ways that made my vision haze.

He hesitated, just for a heartbeat, long enough for me to see the question in his eyes. I answered by rocking my hips, urging him. A growl rumbled through his chest. That single sound turned every nerve in my body to liquid fire.

Then he drove into me, slow at first, letting me adjust. My head fell back, a ragged moan bursting from somewhere deep in my chest. He felt impossibly big, stretching me wide, filling me completely. A strange tension unwound inside me as his thick length slid into my wet heat. It was like part of me had been waiting forever to slot into place with him, a perfect fit.

He buried himself fully with a trembling groan, chest heaving and muscles rippling beneath my fingers. "Selene," he grated out, voice raw with need and emotion.

"Vyne." My fingers found the wiry ridges at his nape, hooking there as I lifted my hips in response. He bit back a curse, pinning me down with strong hands, his grip both possessive and worshipful. My body shivered, and tingles spread along my skin from his touch.

That was all the warning I got before he started moving, a heated rhythm that built and built inside me. His hips rocked and bucked, driving into my core with firm, purposeful strokes. The slick sounds of our joining and our mingled pants and groans filled the air.

With each pass of his hard length, the tension inside me gathered and pulled taut, a coiling spring of building pleasure. I could feel myself growing hotter and wetter around him, my slick walls clenching and fluttering. My sex throbbed, a tight, focused ache that demanded to be filled and scratched.

He pounded into me, each powerful thrust jostling my body, rocking me with his force. That full, stretched feeling of his cock stroking deep grew sharper, more insistent. The drag of him across my senses was deliciously, exquisitely overwhelming. I wanted to be consumed and digested by the consuming pleasure until nothing remained but the infinite, inescapable finish of him.

I fisted a handful of silk, crying out. My climax rolled through me in dizzying waves. I barely came down before he pounded forward one last time, letting out a ragged cry that shook my bones. His wings flared wide, tail lashing against the stone. The sudden burst of warmth deep inside me made my body clamp around him all over again, a final spasm of shared passion.

It took awhile, but we unfurled from that state of frantic bliss, panting like we'd run a marathon. The heat of the room folded in around us, but for once, it didn't feel stifling. Our bodies stuck together with sweat, but I was in no rush to pull away.

His weight pressed into me for a minute, heavy and protective. Then, carefully, he slipped free, leaving my limbs quivering. My face felt hot, but my heart felt strangely light.

He settled at my side, half propped up on an elbow. I laughed under my breath. "I can't feel my legs," I murmured.

"Good," he was all male satisfaction. He reached down, dragging the silks over us, and the subtle thoughtfulness made my chest tighten in a whole different way. A girl could get used to this.

For a while, we lay there, listening to each other breathe. His tail drifted over my leg in a lazy caress.

My gaze landed on Vyne's face. He was watching me with this intensity that could have been intimidating if I didn't know him so well. I traced a faint scar along his collarbone. "I love you, you know," I blurted.

He stilled. For a split second, I wondered if I'd gone too far. Shit. This whole mating thing was too new, too unexpected. Emotions were running high. Endorphins were screwing with my head. I could make a dozen excuses, and none of them would be true.

Then his eyes softened. "I ... I love you too, *Zhyvarin*," he said, so quiet I barely heard it, a secret encapsulated by the rock walls around us.

My throat squeezed. It felt like I'd spent years stumbling through chaos, only to finally land there, wrapped in this Drakarn's arms. My earlier guilt poked at me—there were still so many people outside this room who needed help. But I couldn't argue that this moment was essential, too.

I couldn't do this without Vyne. Without my mate.

When I curled in closer, he tucked me under his chin, a fierce tenderness in the gesture. The last remnants of the tension I was carrying started to bleed away.

"We should rest," he said. "Tomorrow will be ... complicated."

I huffed a wry sound, already imagining the avalanche of tasks waiting. "It's always complicated. But at least I'll have you to help me through it."

My voice was heavy with lingering exhaustion, so the last few words came out tender, almost shy. That was new and startling, but he didn't seem to mind. He pulled the silks tighter around us, sealing in the comforting weight of this private forge filled only with our mingled breath.

I pressed a final kiss to his scaled neck, letting my

eyelids sink shut. Somehow, even amid all the chaos forever swirling in this world, I felt ... safe. It was a luxury I barely felt like I deserved.

Sleep claimed me gently as Vyne's breathing evened out, and my last thought was simple:

Finally, I'd found something worth letting myself fall for.

I made my way through rows of stone beds I knew by heart now, each step a reminder of how hard we'd fought to keep the Drakarn here alive. I heard few raspy breaths and more gentle sighs, and my own pulse eased in response. My fingers automatically brushed table edges to check supplies. But something was different this morning. I felt lighter, steadier.

I could see progress.

The Drakarn who'd been near death two days ago were no longer caught in that frantic half-consciousness. Their scales still lacked their full luster, but there was a definite shimmer there—life returning to their bodies. It was enough to flood my chest with cautious hope.

Mysha was sitting, her back propped up by pillows and her hands cupping a steaming mug. She glared at me as I approached, and I couldn't stop the smile that spread across my face. If she was feeling well enough to glare, she might actually pull through.

"What mess have you made of my healing caverns, human?" Mysha demanded, setting her mug on her bedside table.

"I think that's a question I should be asking you." I sat at the end of her bed, careful to avoid her legs and tail. "We used vyrathis to aid in healing, but I have no idea why you or the other healers got sick. The illness only affected the healers, as best we can tell." I paused for a moment, but she would want to know. "Three died."

Mysha sneered and hissed. "Damnation. How long have I been ill?"

"About two weeks."

She thought for several moments, reaching for her mug and sipping again before setting it back down. "Healer's Fatigue."

"What?" My fingers itched for a notebook, but I wasn't going to leave when Mysha was giving me answers.

"It's an old illness, and rare. I haven't seen it in my lifetime, but my mentor told me about a spell of it that nearly wiped out Scalvaris a century ago. Remnants of illness lurk in all of us, and in healers, it can mount until it reaches a saturation point and transform into something deadly. It first spreads through the healers, then to anyone who helps, then the rest of the city. Vyrathis is the only known treatment. It gives our bodies a chance to fight the illness. I must have told you before I succumbed." She nodded, satisfied with her deduction.

It wasn't exactly right, but close enough that I saw no reason to contradict her. "Will you tell Rachel and Kaiya about this? If you're up for it?"

She tried to swing her legs off the bed. "I'll be up and tending to the sick. They can find me after."

I placed my hand on her leg. "Maybe tomorrow, elder. Your body needs a bit more healing."

She hissed again, but didn't try to stand. She must have been truly fatigued. I left her to her rest.

I spent the next several minutes making check after check. Supplies? Holding out. Pulses? Steady. Fevers? Seemed to be back under control.

I spotted a large silhouette hovering near the beds in the back. Khorlar. His imposing figure blended into the rock—broad shoulders, dark gray scales, wings folded so tightly against his back he almost vanished into the cavern wall. He might have gone unnoticed if I didn't catch the glint of light reflecting off his scales.

He didn't look to me as I approached. Still, I knew he was aware of me; I'd seen his battle instincts firsthand. His wings stayed clamped to his spine, and he stared at a point on the wall like he was trying to memorize every chiseled contour.

"Khorlar?" I kept my voice quiet, not wanting to disturb anyone else who might be sleeping.

He finally glanced my way. His eyes narrowed slightly in acknowledgement. He was silent for an uncomfortable stretch before he answered, "Checking."

I tilted my head. "Things are improving," I said, my tone gentler than I'd expected. "Thank you. We wouldn't have made it back if not for your help." I didn't want to imagine what the Ingarath would have done to us. They hadn't gotten the chance.

He didn't nod, just flicked his tail once against the stone. "I honor my duty," he said. It was so formal, carefully worded. I wondered what he was really doing there. But I doubted he'd welcome more questions.

After a moment, he turned on his heel and prowled to the passageway. He didn't look back.

I didn't have time to waste on mysterious Drakarn.

Reika was right where I'd left her—still frail but getting stronger. Her hollow cheeks and bruises looked less brutal this morning, and her breathing was relaxed, if shallow. She appeared to be healing in slow, steady increments. I knelt beside her, studying the lines of tension that still marred her brow. Even in rest, Reika seemed poised on an invisible edge.

"You're safe here," I whispered. I wasn't sure if I said it for her benefit or mine, but it felt like a necessary vow.

When her fingers twitched against the sheet, my heart gave a tiny leap. I didn't know if there were more humans out there, more Reikas who needed saving. If there were, we would find them. We had to.

I pushed to my feet, rubbing my sweaty palms on my thighs. "Rest easy," I mumbled.

A shuffle near the entrance made me turn. My stiff shoulders loosened when I spotted Vyne, and my cheeks strained with a smile. This thing between us had me looking like a fool.

I didn't care.

"Long shift?" he asked. His voice, that low rumble, always made me feel safer.

"You could say that." My body ached. "But there's progress. Mysha woke up for a bit and was able to explain what happened."

He glanced at the cots the same way I had, that fierce intelligence of his taking in details. "Good. They need you."

Heat prickled across my face, and I was thankful for the murky lighting that might hide how flustered I felt. "I'm just doing what I can." Then, I gestured toward the exit. "I think I've earned a break. Walk me home?"

Vyne offered a smile, the kind that made my heart stutter. He closed the distance, holding out his large, claw-tipped hand. I didn't hesitate, sliding my smaller one into his, and everything inside me clicked into place.

We left, the air outside the cavern cooler, though the city itself never truly cooled. We walked in silence for a while, letting the labyrinthine corridors of Scalvaris swallow us.

"Vega wants to go searching for more humans. She isn't wrong—it's important. I'm guessing the council isn't going to like that." They hadn't when Vega escaped the city to come rescue me and the civilians I was hiding with in a cave not far from our initial crash site. I had no idea how that might have turned out if Terra wasn't snuggled up with their leader.

Being snuggled up to a Drakarn of my own, now I saw the appeal.

His fingers tightened around mine. "They won't," he said. "The Ignarath will demand retribution for the scouts we killed. Sending a human like Vega out anywhere near their territory could court war if she manages to survive."

I cursed. "I don't know if anything can stop Vega, short of throwing her into a cell. And even that didn't work for long."

He released my hand and turned, his broad shoulders blocking some of the corridor's pale glow. "That is not a problem for today, *Zhyvarin*."

I might have argued, but I was tired from my shift and right next to my mate. I didn't want to waste time worrying about Vega and her future.

We walked again and made it to Vyne's—*our*—room. The heavy door slid shut with a stony thump, locking out the noise of the city.

Vyne let go of my hand to undo the leather straps across his chest, removing one layer of armor. His wings came free, then settled behind him. I stared a fraction too long, every inch of him reminding me just how good he looked, and how much he was mine.

"Sit," he ordered gently, gesturing to a cushioned ledge along the wall. I did as asked, too tired to protest. My legs throbbed in relief when I sank into the seat.

He knelt in front of me, massive and graceful. The heat of his scales radiated through my clothes. "You're pushing yourself hard," he said, blunt as ever, though his tone was oddly gentle. One clawed hand lifted, brushing hair away from my face. "You do so much, Selene. For them. For us. Don't lose yourself."

I tried to reply, but I didn't manage more than a shaky exhale. The exhaustion I'd been pushing aside the entire day suddenly crashed down, and I realized I was trembling. Vyne's hands came up to frame my face, holding me steady in a way that seemed to say, I've got you.

"You don't have to say anything," he murmured, pressing his brow to mine. His breath, hot and steady, ghosted over my lips, and his wings flared forward to cocoon us. It was so private, so comforting, that something in my chest cracked open.

When I found my voice, it wobbled. "Thank you," I managed. It felt woefully inadequate, but it was all I had.

Vyne's thumbs rubbed small circles along my jaw. Then he tugged me toward him, arms wrapping around my waist. I fell into his chest, catching the deep, resonant thump of his heart, the scales shifting across his broad shoulders. Every inch of me seemed to unravel in that slow, careful warmth.

"You're mine, *Zhyvarin*," he whispered. "No matter what wars or storms come."

My heart lurched. I pulled back just enough to

see his face, sliding my fingers over the rise of scales on his shoulder. He shivered beneath my touch, eyes slipping half-closed as he leaned into my hand. The trust in his expression nearly undid me.

He guided his mouth to mine, sealing the moment in a slow, tender kiss. No urgency this time, no desperate clash. Just a soft, lingering exchange that tasted of devotion and everything we would build.

I wrapped my arms around him and surrendered.

KHORLAR

I stood perched on a rocky outcropping, arms crossed. Below, trainees sparred with varying degrees of competence, most displaying defensive formations as porous as the atmosphere above Volcaryth. A flicker of impatience ignited in my chest—an instinctive urge to snarl corrections or bark orders. I suppressed it. Not yet. Let them taste failure, scrape their hides raw. They'd learn more from bruises than lectures.

My gaze moved restlessly between sparring pairs, weighing their intent against clumsy execution. Bad habits, unchecked now, would bleed them dry later. A head thrown too far back during a strike, a tail dragging where it should provide balance ... my patience frayed, but remained, for the moment, intact.

Then my gaze drifted, pulled across the cavern to the far side: the humans.

They weren't sparring Drakarn today. Their exercise centered on scaling the treacherous rock faces, navigating the uneven terrain with a painstaking focus. Boots scraped against sharp edges and loose rubble, their small, strange hands finding purchase along jagged holds. Where my kind relied on tails for balance and powerful wings for controlled descents, the humans compensated with an unnerving precision, gripping tighter, crouching lower. It wasn't natural—it couldn't be, for them—but they were relentless.

One caught my attention.

Hair pulled back under a utilitarian leather band, a face that radiated composure despite the exertion evident in every controlled movement. It wasn't unusual for me to observe the humans as they moved through the caverns; curiosity was simply practicality draped in the guise of observation.

But this one ... she was singularly focused. Intent.

She studied the rock face before her as though it were a puzzle to be solved, not merely an obstacle to overcome. A sharpness edged her gaze, darting and aware, registering movement and depth in ways I hadn't noticed in the others.

Without conscious intent, I edged closer to the platform's edge, my breath measured as I watched her ascend. She was precision incarnate ... until she wasn't. One of those leather boots dislodged something loose, a hairline crack spider-webbing across the rock face in an instant.

Then everything happened almost too fast for reaction.

The crack widened, a series of sharp pops and snaps that broadcast disaster as physics caught up. Her hand shot upward, grasping for a higher hold. She didn't scream, didn't freeze, but some instinct drove her to try and stabilize as the rock beneath her gave way.

First, loose stones slammed against the cliff face, falling in an uncontrolled cascade. Then, her body followed, moving too fast. She twisted mid-air, clawing desperately for purchase, but collided hard against another outcropping several feet below. Another slip, a mere inch more, and she'd have plunged off the ledge into oblivion.

The rockfall wasn't stopping. Dust clouded the dim light, obscuring her small, curled form.

"Damn it." The words were a low growl ripped from my throat.

Instinct surged, burning white-hot, obliterating every other thought. My claws scraped against the rock as I launched myself forward. Survival demanded timing, precise calculation—not reckless action—and yet there I was, abandoning calculation entirely.

My kind did not make mistakes on terrain like this. My hands gripped the heated rock, tighter than iron, carving a path downward with an unforgiving mix of force and control. The stones that had crumbled toward her still rained around us.

Her scent hit then. Even amidst the acrid chaos of dust and falling debris, it struck me like a whip. I refused to acknowledge the sensory jolt, the sudden hypersensitivity that flared on my tongue.

Everything sharpened, refocused, as though a lightning bolt had struck me.

Her scent was closer now: crisp and alien, deceptively light, yet sharp enough to draw blood. Beneath the atmospheric noise of the cavern, I could almost hear the frantic beat of her pulse—faint but rapid, defying her outward composure.

The last few feet were the most treacherous. Sharp stones forced an awkward perch, wings momentarily extending for balance as dirt and gravel shifted. Any lesser warrior would pause, regroup, resist the urge to charge blindly.

No time for that.

Seconds mattered. Less than that.

Then she was there—fingers white-knuckling a warped, unstable ledge that offered no real security. A smear of blood at her knuckles. A precarious over-hang threatened to collapse near her left leg. I landed close, but not close enough, not yet at her side.

This place offered no kindness, no quarter.

"Don't move!" My voice thundered, an imperative, not a request.

Everything else dissolved as I extended my clawed hand to her. Any sweetness lingering beneath her scent was ruthlessly ignored, my focus narrowing to necessary efficiency as I sought a more secure foothold. The chaos subsided, leaving lingering instability in its wake.

I pulled her away from the ledge.

The world narrowed to the visceral—the grit of her bloodied hands slipping against my claws, the searing heat of the broken rock, her weight against my grip. Every sense screamed for focus, demanding I lock down instinct and channel it into precision.

The tension ratcheted tighter, some unseen thread pulling at a place I hadn't had time to name—something wild and ancient, testing the limits of my control as her scent flooded the space between us, closer this time. My tongue burned as if branded, the acrid metallic tang of danger mingling with her phantom sweetness.

This was not the moment for distraction—damned if my own body didn't agree—but the sensation was suffocating, scalding. It deepened as I wrapped my other clawed hand around her waist, sharp focus overriding any resistance. No matter how fast I worked, the heat radiating off her lingered, clinging to me.

"You weigh less than an ash cat," I grunted, hauling her upward. "Stop fighting me."

"I'm not fighting!" she hissed, her voice sharper than expected. She kicked her legs toward the collapsing rubble below, struggling for a foothold. I swore and pulled harder, drawing her body flush against mine.

"Then stop squirming!" I snapped.

The moment her weight fully shifted into my grasp, the tension snapped—not just in the rock, but somewhere deeper. My tail flicked against the ledge as I propelled us upward, clearing the worst of the debris. My wings flared briefly, catching the air to stabilize us, and finally—finally—we landed on solid footing.

Her breath hitched, the first unguarded sound of emotion slipping past her carefully constructed exterior. For a moment, we were utterly still. Dust settled in the faint light, coating her bruised and dirt-streaked skin like motes of gold.

Her scent lingered. Unforgivingly.

"Are you injured?" My voice was gruff, harsher than intended.

Her chest rose and fell rapidly. She tilted her head, those sharp, assessing eyes locking onto mine as though calculating some equation that couldn't be spoken aloud.

"Nothing broken," she rasped, exhaustion evident in her tone. "Thanks."

There it was—a flicker, a crack barely noticeable, as if she'd loosened her grip on the vigilance she wore like armor. When her fingers brushed briefly against the clawed hand still gripping her waist, I felt her relax.

That wouldn't do. Not here. Not now.

Not with *her*.

"Be more careful next time," I ground out, my voice cracking like a whip. Without ceremony, I released her, the distance I needed achieved as she staggered to her feet. She didn't fall, though; her legs steadied quickly, and she held herself like a queen.

Her expression shifted imperceptibly, mouth settling into its former sharp line. The momentary vulnerability I'd glimpsed dissolved as quickly as it had appeared.

Good. Better this way.

She took a breath, her jaw working as if considering something to say before closing her mouth again. Straightening her spine, she moved stiffly past, her scent trailing after her like smoke.

I stood rooted, my chest tightening under the weight of it all—her scent, the phantom warmth of her body pressed against mine, the impossible ache that clawed through me like something ancient trying to awaken.

It couldn't awaken. It wouldn't.

The burn on my tongue refused to fade.

Khorlar's story is coming soon!

Thank you so much for reading *Scorched by Fate*!

Your support means the world to me. If you enjoyed the story, it would mean even more if you could take a moment to share your thoughts in a review or leave a rating.

Hearing from readers like you makes all the difference!

Need a little more of Vyne & Selene?

Sign up at the link below to **receive a free bonus epilogue!**

Get your freebie!
https://katerudolph.net/index.php/vyne-bonus/

AVAILABLE IN KINDLE UNLIMITED
FOR A LIMITED TIME

Exile's Hunter

Kenzie will do anything to save her sister... even if it means teaming up with a dangerous alien who makes her heart pound.

Kenzie has crossed the galaxy in search of her abducted sister and she's finally landed on Guerran. It's a planet full of criminals and she can trust no one, especially not the terrifyingly hot alien named Mad.

He's as much a criminal as anyone on Guerran. And he's her only hope. But she isn't sure whether she should kiss him or stab him when his presence makes her heat up with desire.

Mad can't leave the exile planet. Once Kenzie finds Carise, the sisters will be long gone. There's no future between her and the hunky alien, no matter how quickly he steals her heart.

How can Kenzie walk away when fate has put her in the path of her mate?

Exile's Adored

Help isn't coming.

When Carise wakes up on an alien planet running is her only chance at escape, even if being caught means death.

She'd rather die than face whatever her captors plan to do to her.

Guerran is no safe place for healing and every moment is fear. Until Jaek, a gentle giant of an alien, makes himself her protector. But when their fragile bond is tested, Carise knows she must find strength within herself to become brave enough to survive Guerran.

This time she won't let herself be taken. And she's not leaving her mate behind.

Dragon Brides
Dragon Princes. Fierce Women. Love.
Fated mates, fierce women, and dragon princes are
ready to find their mates.

Crux
Ranger
Saber
Cipher
Storm
Drake
Asher
Knox
Flint
Pine

Guarded by the Shifter

Werewolf. Bodyguard. Mate.
The origins of these shifters are shrouded in mystery,
but they're determined to protect their mates from
any harm that comes their way.
Also available in audio!
Hunting Season
On the Prowl
Stalking Magic
Hungry for the Wolf
Wolf Cursed (novella)
Wolf's Temptation

Stealing the Alpha

**The thief takes what she wants, but the
alpha keeps what's his...**
Join shifter thief Mel as she clashes with lion alpha
Luke in an explosive trilogy of two opposites who
can't keep away from one another.
Also available in audio!
The Alpha Heist
Entangled with the Thief
In the Alpha's Bed

Alien Mates: Planet Exile

Guerran is no place for pretty human women. But these alien heroes will protect their mates!
Also available in audio!

Exile's Hunter
Exile's Adored

Zulir Warrior Mates

Kidnapped humans. Alien Warriors. Electric wings.
The Zulir Warrior Mates series brings you human heroines and heroes abducted from Earth who find love – and wings! – with the alien warriors who rescue them.
Also available in audio!

Synnr's Saint
Synnr's Hope
Synnr's Spark
Synnr's Kiss
Synnr's Ride

Mated to the Alien

Fated Mate Alien Romance

Detyens are doomed to die young if they don't find their fated mates.

Follow along as these mated pairs fight off aliens, corrupt dictators, prejudiced humans, pirates, and more! The books can be read or listened to in any order, though some characters show up in multiple stories.

Select books available in audio.

Pick a book and jump into the action today!

Ruwen

Tyral

Stoan

Cyborg

Krayter

Kayleb

Shayn

Braxtyn

Doryan

Dekon

Detyen Warriors

Detya was destroyed a hundred years ago. These doomed warriors are out to find justice... and their mates.

The Detyen Warriors series brings you kick butt heroines, alpha alien heroes, fated mates, and relationships strong enough to span the galaxy!

The entire series is also available in audio!

Soulless

Ruthless

Heartless

Faultless

Endless

Detyen Warrior Outcasts
Fated Mate Alien Romance

These doomed warriors were abandoned by their people and live on the edge. Their mates hold the key to their salvation.

Pick a book and jump into the action today!

Dangerous Bond

Intrepid Bond

Wayward Bond

Alien Holiday Romance

Christmas... in space????
These alien holiday romances look beyond Earth's winter holidays and ring in the season across the galaxy!
Select titles available in audio.
Snowed in with the Alien Beast
The Alien's Winter Gift
The Alien Reindeer's Wild Ride
Trapped with her Alien Mate

Alien Outlaws

Outlaws, schemes, and love... it's all there in the Alien Outlaws series...

Andie Munster is sick of life on Ixilta, the planet she got dumped on after being abducted from Earth six years ago. And when the mysterious and dangerous Xandr shows up looking for a way off the planet,

she's half-prisoner, half-co-conspirator in a wild rush
to escape.

Rogue Alien's Escape
Rogue Alien's Woman
Rogue Alien's Secret
Rogue Alien's Legacy

Find more by Kate Rudolph at www.
katerudolph.net

ABOUT KATE RUDOLPH

Kate Rudolph is a paranormal and sci-fi romance writer who lives in Indiana. She loves writing about kick butt heroines and the steamy heroes who love them. She's been devouring romance novels since she was too young to be reading them and had to hide her books so no one would take them away. She couldn't imagine a better job in this world than writing romances and sharing them with her fellow readers.

If you enjoyed this story, please consider leaving a review.